The Crownbound Series
Book One
A Crown Between Shadows
by
Holly Crowe

Published by Pomegranate & Spice Press
Written by Holly Crowe
http://www.hollycroweauthor.com

Cover design by Angie Fernot - @afernot
ISBN: 979-8-9938868-0-0

Dedicated to anyone who grew up writing and never thought anything would come from it.
Keep going.

Chapter 1

Belle never understood how anyone could enjoy attending these events. They were stuffy, stiff, and soaked in pretension to say the very least. With a well-practiced sweep of her hand across the side of her neck, she allowed her long brown hair to fall behind her bare shoulder, exposing her skin as if it were a weapon. They always presented these annoying shows of wealth in a shiny wrapper, and slapped words like 'charity' on it. Belle couldn't think of a single time growing up bouncing between orphanages and foster homes that some rich asshole's charity work had done anything for her.

Ivory, Belle's handler of sorts, had been unnervingly insistent that she take this job; not only for the obscene payout they would get for it, but for some unknown reason that Ivory wouldn't explain. The ticket for this evening's spectacle had been part of the deal, sealed into the contract the moment Belle agreed to take the job. It said something specific to her that this wasn't just a job. Whoever it was that hired her, they didn't just want the necklace that she was sent for; they needed it.

Belle hadn't bothered to look up the ticket's cost, but she could guess. The thick cardstock, golden foil, and was practically gaudy enough to choke on. Belle would never step foot in a place like this for fun. However, for the payout waiting on the other side? With that many zeroes? Hell, she was already planning which island she'd disappear to once the necklace changed hands. Something with blue water. And alcohol, lots of alcohol.

Still... Ivory's voice had been different when she had pushed Belle to take the offer. Almost strained. Almost like the job was personal to them.

Belle offered a polite nod to the guard at the door who took her ticket. The whispers started the moment she crossed the threshold into the grand foyer. All the women were in modest gowns in muted colors, hiding behind layers of fabric, wrapped in silk and subtlety. And then there was Belle. Would it have been smarter to blend in? Wear something demure, disappear into the crowd, just in case things went sideways? Definitely. But blending in was never her style. If she was going to crash a party full of people playing pretend, she'd do it in a red dress that clung to her like a second skin, and with every eye in the room watching her do it.

The dress was strapless with a plunging sweetheart neckline, hugging every curve before loosening at the thigh in a daring slit. The fabric shimmered as she moved, rippling to the floor in waves of silken red, studded with crystalline beads. It was, to Belle, the dress every woman in the room wished she had the nerve to wear instead of their Sunday-best-on-Hollywood-Boulevard gowns. It confused Belle to think about how a color could both be pastel and pale at the same time, and even moreso confusing to her was how at least one third of the women here were all wearing the exact same color.

"You are always such a sight..."

A deep, familiar, and just a touch amused voice snagged Belle mid-step as she strolled by a glittering vase that she had no real interest in. Turning to face the man, she tilted her head up slowly, her hair cascading down her exposed back. "Belle..." His lips curled into a slow, familiar smile, his dark grey eyes pinning her in place. She pursed her lips ever so slightly, allowing her old acquaintance to drink her in because he was, and they both knew it.

Belle could practically feel his gaze trailing over her, slow and hungry. It made her want to shiver. The way that he looked at her, as if he would eat her up, as if he hadn't done so many times in the past. "Donovan Hightower..." she purred, her eyes flaring. "What an... unpleasant... surprise..." A playful smile danced on her lips. "What on earth could you be doing here?" He tipped his chin in that infuriating way that she

2

remembered, then offered her his arm. Belle took it with well-practiced grace and allowed him to lead her through the room.

"I assume the same thing that you are..." She gave a dismissive wave of her hand. "I do hope we won't be bidding on the same item." They shared the common knowledge that neither of them was there to waste time in a room surrounded by people with the same idea of how to measure their own dick size. These people thought that with a tiny paddle showing off how much money they were willing to spend on items that they couldn't take to the grave with themselves showed their importance. Belle allowed Donovan to lead their little journey through the room for now; they stopped periodically at different items, making it seem as if they were interested in what they were looking at; both playing their parts as interested rich people here to spend a ton of money on random pieces of art.

"Donovan, even if we are... We both know I will be long gone before you even have a chance." She added a little shrug before he gripped her arm a little tighter.

"I remember... You do seem to be very adept at walking away..." There was a dull sting in the way that he said it, and the intended hit landed on target, twisting a metaphorical knife in Belle's chest. They had grown up together, both ending up back in the same orphanage when the foster homes inevitably did not work out for one reason or another. They both grew up knowing what it was like to feel unwanted, what it felt like to have people constantly leaving their lives. It is what made them grow closer to each other. It was the base of the relationship that grew between them as they became adults. Their joint knowledge of survival is what brought them both into the same line of work.

They played the same game, but each by a different set of rules. Belle was of the mindset of getting the job done by any means necessary. Donovan was much more of the type to color as close to in the lines as he could for being a thief. "Oh... we're feeling spicy tonight, are we, Donovan?" Despite the ice in her words, her cheeks slowly turned red, a small sign of the lack of true composure over the jab that Donovan hurled at her. Clearing her throat, she angled toward Donovan, removing her arm from his. "Here... Let me add insult to injury, then. At least you'll get to watch me walk away this time..." She smiled, turned on her heel, and walked away, surely leaving him seething.

She shook her head slightly as she walked away, being sure to add a little more sway to her hips than normal, giving Donovan one final show. She'd had the blueprints of the building for weeks now, and the internal setup from posing as a staff member who helped coordinate the event itself. Belle knew the layout better than her own reflection, every hallway, every guard rotation, every blind spot. When no one was looking, Belle slipped through a set of closed doors and quietly walked around the room that was full of various antiquities, vases, paintings, and statues. Eventually, she found the jewelry. She had received a rough sketch of the item that she was looking for in her packet upon agreeing to take the job. A thick silver chain with an ornate silver key attached to it, a rather large red gemstone affixed to the center of it, threads of silver encasing it in place, holding it to the heart of the key.

If her timing was correct, she had a few minutes to spare, while all the patrons were gathered in the main room and the opening announcements were made. Then there would be a near constant flow of stewards bringing items out to be bid upon and back in once they were sold.

"Don't touch it, Belle..."

Goddamnit, Donovan, she thought to herself while huffing out a frustrated breath. Something in his tone brought her to pause; it wasn't just a threat because the necklace was what he was here for. He almost sounded worried for Belle, afraid for her even.

"You cannot possibly be here for this... Whoever hired me would not have hired both of us..." She stepped up to the case, pulling out a small pair of gloves that she had tucked at a garter on her thigh. Donovan slowly closed the distance; his hands tucked into his grey dress slacks.

"I wasn't hired for this one..." He mumbled, dark eyes shifting between the necklace and Belle.

"Oh, honey, for me?" She feigned innocence while bringing a hand to her chest before shifting and waving it dismissively. "I don't have time for you, Donovan." With her gloves on, she lifted the lid on the glass case, allowing it to lean

4

back on the hinges. As she reached for the chain, he reached out and smacked her on the back of the hand, causing Belle to gasp and recoil. "What the fuck, Donovan?"

"I told you not to touch it, Belle. It's not what you think it is." She grumbled out a frustrated breath and unlatched the chain. Donovan let out a string of curses while grabbing her wrist just as her gloved hand came around the key.

She attempted to jerk her hand away from him but froze in place as a strange gust of wind rushed around them, whipping Belle's hair in all directions. It circled them, white smoke wrapped around, blurring anything outside of its path, and then, suddenly the little back room full of items and antiquities that would likely sell for millions of dollars at the end of the night vanished.

They were left in a field, grass as far as the eye could see, and the bright sun above them, breeze carrying the scent of spring and flowers. Her heels began to sink into the grass under her. "What the fuck, Donovan?" Belle yanked her hands away from him, holding the key firmly in her gloved hands. She watched as he shook his head and took a step back, running his hands through his now windblown hair. Already growing tired of her heels sinking into the ground, she bent and took them off before storming over to Donovan, straps to her shoes in one hand, the key locked in a death grip in the other. "What... the... fuck..." She repeated, tone pointed and accusatory, eyes wide as she stared at him. "Where the fuck are we? What the hell just happened?"

"Home..." He huffed out a breath before scrubbing his hands over his face. "Belle, I told you not to touch the fucking thing." He was doing his best not to shout at her. Instead, he stepped away, letting out a yell of frustration. Donovan spun back to her quickly and held his hand out toward her; a vine of black smoke extended from his palm, and the key she was holding so tightly onto vanished from her hand, and when the smoke dissipated, the key was gone. Donovan rolled his shoulders feeling his natural magic coursing through his body for the first time in a very long time. It trickled through every inch of his body from head to toe. Having not used his power for so long, all he could hope for was that the key was sent somewhere safe. Her jaw dropped, eyes wide and fixed on him, but he didn't have time to explain, not here, not now. "We have to get out of here..." He muttered, grabbing her by the wrist, attempting to pull her with him.

"No!" She shouted, yanking her arm back, the glove slipping from her hand before falling to the grass between them as she took a few careful steps away from him. "You need to tell me what the hell is going on. What was..." She wildly gestured to his hand, wiggling her fingers, "That. What was that?" She yelled after him when he turned his back on her and started storming away. Using her free hand, she grabbed the length of the dress and picked it up, allowing herself to walk faster to catch up with him. Stumbling after Donovan, Belle couldn't help but throw her heels over her shoulders, attempting to scratch an itch that formed deep in the center of her back. One of those down to the root itches that slowly drove you mad.

There was a sharp noise, somewhere between a hiss and a whistle, quickly followed by Donovan's body lurching forward before he dropped to his knee. Deep red liquid splashed down onto the lush green grass, "Shit..." He grunted, and Belle screamed, running to him. Donovan once again grabbed her wrist, trying to pull her with him as he forced himself upright and trudged forward.

There were two more sharp sounds, and Donovan yanked roughly at Belle's arm, tucking her in front of him as one of the arrows struck the back of his leg, and the other jutted through the front of his shoulder from the back, nearly clipping Belle as well, A small splat of blood covered Belle's bare shoulder. "Little brother..." The voice seemed to come from nowhere and everywhere at once; low, amused, and laced with menace. The air split with a quick woosh, and three dark portals opened around them, trapping them in the center as Donovan fell to his knees once more, pulling Belle down with him, practically under him. Her bottom lip trembled, and her hands shook as she reached toward Donovan, the length of the bright red dress puddling around her. He snapped the back of the arrow in his leg off before yanking it through the front with a guttural yell, shoving the blood-soaked arrow tip into Belle's hand, giving her even a tiny whisper of a prayer to combat what was likely about to come.

6

There was too much happening for Belle to take it all in at once. Donovan was grunting and groaning, having been shot with a total of three arrows now. There were three large, swirling black portals, wind whipping through them even as guards stepped through. The guards were dressed in black metallic armor, and they moved methodically, trapping Belle and Donovan in the center of the circle they formed. "Little brother..." The voice repeated, "You've brought a human back to our realm with you? Naughty boy..." The tall man at the center chided Donovan before pulling his helmet off. As if Belle had not already lived through multiple impossible things in the last ten minutes, the man beneath the helmet was the spitting image of Donovan. Her Donovan, little orphan Donovan that had grown up with her, had a brother, and not only was this man that was hovering over them Donovan's brother, but he was Donovan's twin.

"No..." The word all but purred from the twin as he nodded for the guards to pick Belle up off the ground. Survival instincts kicked in immediately, and she began to flail, screaming like a banshee while bringing her hand down in rough, quick, stabbing motions with the tip of the arrow. Her first attempt bounced off armor at the guard's forearm with a metallic clang, but her second downward stab landed with a squelching noise of blade breaking flesh. The guard reared back and aimed to slap Belle across the face for the assault, but the twin flicked his wrist, and the guard was sent flying back through the portal. "No, little brother... This feral thing... she's not human, is she?" With a small movement of his wrist, dark smoke, like what she had just witnessed from Donovan, wrapped around Belle, trapping her hands to her sides and binding her ankles together.

Donovan took a slow, unsteady breath in, the arrow that lodged through his shoulder may have been low enough to clip his lung. "Davion, get away from her..." He grumbled weakly while trying to push himself to his feet. The twin, now known as Davion, laughed and shoved the heel of his booted foot into Donovan's shoulder, knocking him back to the ground.

"Get away from him!" Belle screamed. Davion cocked his head to the side slightly before crouching over his injured brother. Drawing a small blade from his boot, his dark eyes locked onto Belle. "I will fucking kill you." She threatened, even though she was restrained by some weird force that she had no idea what to do with. Davion's lips curled into a fiendish smile as he stabbed the blade down into Donovan's leg, straight through to the dirt below. "Where's the key?" Davion barked. Donovan screamed and swung out to punch his brother, but Davion was already back on his feet. Turning his attention back to Belle now that he knew Donovan wouldn't be going anywhere.

"It's already gone, Davion," Donovan bellowed before reaching for the blade in his leg, trying to pull it out, but he was growing weaker by the second. He didn't even have the strength to sit up, but he forced himself to be as steady as he could.

"What a loud woman... Curious..." Davion towered over Belle, quietly amused by her struggling against the magic that held her in place. He took a glove off his right hand and tried to place it on her cheek. Belle attempted to lash out and bite him before she jerked away. So instead, Davion grabbed her jaw, framing it in his large hand while forcing her to look back at him. He continued to move her, tilting her head to the side as he leaned in closer to take a slow, controlled breath in at her neck.

As if whatever he found there shook him to his core, the bindings on Belle faltered, even if only for a second, and that was all she needed. With her arms free, she lashed out, slapping him hard enough across the face to snap his neck sideways. Her nails had pulled across his face in the process, cutting him twice, leaving two thin red lines on his cheek. Even as the bindings snapped back into place, now around her wrists, binding them closely to one another, he didn't retaliate. He simply righted himself, standing tall. "I see..." A slow, amused smile formed across his lips before he looked at one of his guards. "Bring her with us."

Shifting his gaze once more. "Kill him." He pointed at Donovan, and Belle screamed again, pushing against her restraints even as a guard picked her up in the middle, draping her over his shoulder. She pounded against the guard's armor, fists slamming uselessly into steel. When she bucked her hips, his grip only tightened, locking her in place as they stepped

8

through the portal of dark smoke just in time to see two guards crowd around Donovan, and then there was just darkness; just the smoke that consumed all the light around her.

Chapter 2

The guards unceremoniously dropped Belle on a couch in the room that occupied the other side of the portal. The small group of them turned and left as quickly and as quietly as they could, as if they knew there was more threat to them inside the room rather than outside of it. Davion stepped through the portal and the bindings at Belle's wrists and ankles vanished. She looked down at her wrists for a second before she sprang to her feet and sprinted forward, crystals on her dress glittering in the dim light of the room as she aimed for the portal just on the other side of Davion. She had to go back to Donovan; she had to save him.

Davion calmly pivoted aside as she bolted toward the portal. His hands folded behind his back. With an almost imperceptible flick of his wrist the portal snapped closed within a breath of her reaching it. He watched her slide to a stop, her shoulders sagging in defeat. To the far side of the room, another door opened, and two women rushed in. Davion held his arms out to the side and the women set to work removing his armor. None of them seemed phased when Belle let out a scream in frustration, before storming back toward Davion. "You are a fucking coward." She snapped at him, jabbing an accusatory finger at him while closing the distance.

The women finished removing the armor and gathered it in their arms before leaving the room just as quietly as they came in. Davion towered over Belle now, more man than soldier, in a black loose fitted shirt and black pants, his feet bare. The look on his face was unimpressed as Belle shoved at his chest, forcing him to take a step back. "How could you just leave him

10

there? What on earth would make you want to kill your own brother, you... you..." She was so angry, so overwhelmed, so beyond words. Belle's chest heaved as she searched for words, allowing an uncomfortable silence to fester between them.

Davion was losing his patience, unaccustomed to having anyone talk back to him outside of his mother, the Queen. He had learned from a very young age to just take verbal abuse from her. Belle opened her mouth to keep going, but he didn't shout. He didn't move. He just looked at her. Smoke, thick and black, poured from the air and coiled around her throat. Her breath caught as the vine-like magic cinched tighter, snapping her mouth shut while it slithered up to gag her. Panic surged, but so did fury. "Before you invent new ways to insult me, or damn me to a thousand hells, perhaps you would like to hear my side of the story?" He offered, while retreating slightly, to buy himself some distance from her jabbing finger. Davion approached a small dark wooden table, covered in ornate glass bottles. "I am going to make you a drink." He held his hands up defensively, as if to show her that he meant no harm, despite the thick smoke cutting off her airway. "I believe your world calls it alcohol." He watched as her eyes shifted between him and the small table that he had approached.

He poured two glasses, intentionally taking his time, as if waiting to see the rage dissipate from her face. Instead... When Davion looked at her, he saw the color drain from her face, just in time to see her eyes roll, and her body go limp. "Graces..." he muttered while flicking his wrist out, the small snake of smoke that had covered her neck shifted, and expanded, enveloping Belle and cradling her back to the couch. He allowed the smoke to retreat after he had settled her onto the couch. He narrowed his eyes slightly while watching as Belle brought a hand to her chest as if coaching herself to steady her breathing.

Davion sat on the couch opposite her, placing her glass on the table between them. Belle looked down at the glass on the table and then looked back at Davion, arching a brow as she tipped her chin up slightly. "I saved you from my brother. I would not poison you." In a small movement of what Davion perceived as defiance, Belle crossed her arms over her chest, and he couldn't help but notice the way that the movement pushed up on her breasts. Clearing his throat, he leaned forward and reached for her glass, taking a sip before putting it back down on the table with a slightly more forceful thud. They stared each other down as Belle leaned in and grabbed the glass, downing the brown liquid in one go. "Magnificent..." he practically purred while settling back in the chair across from Belle, a grin forming. He watched her back straighten before her shoulders rolled, something he had seen her do at least three times now.

"Talk." She demanded while adjusting herself on the couch, having nearly forgotten she was in an elegant evening gown, in contrast to Davion, who now just looked like he was in relaxing clothes. Her mind was still racing faster than she could fully comprehend, but if she got him talking, he was distracted, and if he was distracted, she could process or maybe even formulate a plan.

"My name is Prince Davion Hightower. My parents are Queen Martine and the departed King Davion..." He paused for a split second, "Our parents, as it were, Donovan and I. Donovan escaped to your realm many, many years ago and took with him a valuable key. One that allows our kind to travel across the two different realms." As much as Belle was hoping that he would just talk, so that she could drown him out and process, he had her attention. She found herself tilting her head to the side slightly, taking in Davion's features, comparing them to Donovan's. Her heart ached, and the sting of tears started to form before Belle forced herself to be present. "Donovan took the key so that our mother, Queen Martine, would be unable to unite the realms. He took it and ran from us, locking our only way into your realm. I assume that you found the key, it activated when it was touched, and you somehow have some amount of fae blood in you, or the key would have just been a key. You brought a traitor back into our realm, and he had to be dealt with."

She scratched the back of her neck and spared a second to look at her empty glass before returning to Davion. He had been watching her, studying her every movement; his dark eyes followed hers and, with a little sigh, he rolled his arm, leisurely, and the dark smoke formed and carried two bottles to them, setting them on the table between them. Belle leaned forward

12

and poured herself another glass, her chest rising high with a forced, unnatural control. Her free hand motioned with a rounding gesture of her wrist, motioning for Davion to continue.

As she looked up to Davion, she noticed that he tensed slightly. "Oh, that's right. Royalty. Probably not used to a random commoner demanding that you do anything." She sat back on the couch with her glass in hand now, crossing one leg over the other, the red fabric falling back, exposing both of her legs. "Would you rather I kneel and beg?" She saw his jaw tense and relax, while his eyes darkened for just a moment. Internally, she cursed her own sarcastic, loud-mouthed nature. What the hell was she doing? Trying to flirt with the man who just ordered her best friend to be murdered? If she stopped to think and mourn, Belle was silently convinced that she would be dead just like Donovan.

Survival. It was the only thought that kept repeating through her head. Survive. It repeated in its varying forms. You can survive this. Belle kept repeating in her mind. There would be another time to grieve, other times to weep; but for now, she just needed to survive. To steady her nerves, Belle wrapped her fingers around the glass, holding onto it as if it were her lifeline.

"I'm not used to... really... anyone being so blunt around me. It is generally all bows, curtsies, manners, and such." He refilled his own glass, "As for your... demand..." he mimicked her circular wrist movement, reclining back in his chair. "Donovan was the younger of us; it made him incredibly unhappy knowing that I was rightfully next in line for the throne, and that I had been given all the training on how to rule as the next generation when the time came, and he was trained to simply be my guard. His bitter feelings got the best of him; he escaped with the key to your realm and has been hiding there." He shook his head before pointing one finger at Belle while still holding the glass, balancing it on the arm of the chair. "What I do not understand is where you fit into the picture with my brother."

Belle's cheeks had started to feel warm, and undoubtedly flushed thanks to the alcohol that she assumed he was attempting to ply her with. Admittedly, Belle would allow his attempt because it was calming her nerves. His quizzical tone

13

made Belle tilt her head slightly to the side. "We move in the same circles... In my world..." She mocked his tone while looking over at him. "Answer me this, princeling... How is it that he was able to have the knowledge of the keys and steal the key into my world as a seven-year-old boy? When I met him, he just seemed so out of place, a kid trying..." She trailed off, watching as the full-grown man in front of her began to shift. He aged, in reverse, becoming smaller and younger, until he was a spitting image of the little dark-haired boy that she had met twenty years ago. "What the fuck..." She muttered while sitting straight again, finishing off the glass of alcohol that she had in her hand and placing it on the table between them.

"We can change our appearance at will. I assume that a lost little boy would garner more sympathy than a grown man thrown into a strange world with hardly any knowledge of it... Certainly, my brother was tactical enough to assume the same." As he spoke, he began to shift back, voice aging with him, beginning with the tone of a seven-year-old boy, and ending as the grown man before her once more. "He was a very clever man, too smart for his own good; he would use anyone and anything he could to serve his purpose."

"Why kill him? Why not bring him back here and make him pay for his supposed crimes?" Belle offered while studying Davion, intentionally leaving him room to answer. She noticed the differences between the two men. Donovan always had shaggy hair that curled slightly, and Davion kept his hair shorter, pushed back from his face. Davion had a small scar on his cheek, which was perpendicular to the two red scratches he wore now; Donovan had only gotten into fights when it was necessary and normally came away unscathed.

Belle's false bravado started to slip as she thought about the blood, the screams, and the smoke... It played on repeat behind her eyes like a curse she couldn't blink away.

"Oh, woman, I did not kill him..." his tone grew dark, so did his eyes as he leveled them on Belle's. "His blood is not on my hands, nor my heart. Killing him there was a mercy in comparison to what the queen would have in store for him." Davion leaned forward and refilled both of their glasses. "My turn..." He held her glass out to her, silently urging her to continue drinking, "What do I call you?" His tone softened

14

and his head tilted to the side slightly, taking his time to study her now, drinking her in like what Donovan had done back at the gala.

"My name is Belle." She grabbed the glass and balanced it on her knee as she sat back. "Why didn't you kill me too? Why bring me here? What is the plan with me going forward? I'm no use to you."

"You were uninjured." He gave a slight shrug before sitting back in his chair. "There was no need for you to watch the traitor die when you had no idea of his crimes. You would get a sour taste for me without knowing all the details." He took a sip, eyeing Belle as if to tell her to do the same. Her eyes narrowed, and she tapped her nails along the glass, but did not drink. "Also... I don't think any person in this realm would willingly, and competently be able to teach you about the magic that your blood truly holds..." He had her there... He had, on more than one occasion, mentioned that she wasn't all human, that she had fae blood; did that mean she could control smoke like she had seen him do? "Admittedly, you were also stunning, and I am a man after all."

There it was. She shook her head slightly and grinned, slowly inhaling. "And is that the trade rolling around in your mind? You teach me what I can do, I... what... get on my knees for you?" Uncrossing her legs, she pushed herself to her feet, downing the amber liquid in one go once more before slamming the glass down on the table. "Drink up, princeling, it takes a lot more than fancy booze to get me naked." She added a mock curtsey before beginning to move around the space. Granted, she had no idea where she would go, but she needed to move.

His hand snapped out, catching her jaw before she could move. Belle hadn't even seen him stand, but there he was, circling the small table between them, closing the distance like a storm. He tilted her head back, forcing her to look up at him. "The women of this realm do not have the spark that you do, Belle." His thumb brushed against her jaw as he leaned in, voice low and deliberate. "As for the removal of your clothes..." She clamped her hand around his wrist, nails digging in deep. A warning. A promise. Her glare could've cracked stone. His eyes roamed over her face, slow and possessive, as if

15

memorizing every freckle. "Then I'll just have to try harder, won't I?" 'Intoxicating' didn't even begin to cover the pull that he felt toward her. It was magnetic, dangerous, a gravity all its own.

"You'll fail." With a quick motion, she dipped her head and shoved his hand up, biting down roughly on the webbing between his index finger and thumb. Davion cursed and withdrew from her, rearing back to slap her. He stopped in his tracks when he saw that she didn't flinch, didn't move a single muscle, as if daring him to do it. "Pussy..." She whispered before shaking her head. She had taken her fair share of beatings growing up; a backhand from a man was a normal Friday to Belle at one point.

Davion growled and shouted something in a language that Belle didn't recognize. Almost instantly, two women rushed into the room, stopping in front of him and bowing their heads. "Take our guest to her quarters, see that she is cleaned, clothed, and comforted. Fed too, I would imagine." His tone was rough, demanding, "We will resume this conversation over breakfast in the morning on the back terrace." They nodded at his instruction, and then Davion stomped off.

Belle bit down roughly on her cheek, doing her best to hide her smile. She won the first battle. She proved that the little princeling had never had anyone talk to him how she did, or even strike him, and Belle would use that to her advantage.

"This way, m'lady." Belle shifted her eyes, looking to the more petite of the two women as she piped up. With a small shrug, she nodded and motioned the women forward, following them. What else was she going to do? Fight two little women and then run wildly through a castle that was surely bound to be more of a maze to try to escape into a foreign place with only who knew what kind of threats. Threats, that to the locals would seem normal, but to Belle could be anything.

The stone room they had been in now seemed small in comparison to the rest of the castle. The two women buzzed with energy as they guided Belle through halls, through grand rooms, and up various flights of stairs. They chirped about this and that, the gardens were this way, the main hall was over there; her quarters would be up this way. It seemed never ending. Belle tried to look for anything that could be an exit,

16

something that would at least send her out to the gardens, where she had some sort of chance at getting the hell out of here. Silently chiding herself for such a stupid idea, she shook her head and took a few quick steps to catch up to the women. It would be the most stupid thing for her to try to escape. She had nothing. No friends, no allies, no idea; and a scent that branded her as both human and not; she didn't imagine that Davion was lying when he said that no one would help her learn what she could do. Then there was the thought of what on earth she could do, and why she couldn't do it before?

When they finally came to a stop, Belle forced herself back to reality, if that's what all of this could be called. They were standing in a bedroom the size of her entire apartment. A grand four post bed draped in dark blue and black fabric, colors mirrored by the dark couch and blue chairs that framed a large fireplace with decorative carvings in the stone around the hearth. "This way, m'lady." They led her past the couches, around the bed, and through a smaller set of double doors. "How do we..." The larger of the two women tilted her head slightly while staring at the red dress that hugged Belle.

"Oh no... No..." She wrapped her hands around her torso and took a step back. "I can bathe myself." Belle nodded to the large stone tub, a small swimming pool in her opinion, steaming with hot water. Both women looked at each other before shaking their heads and looking back at Belle.

"We apologize, but the master has given us clear instructions to make sure that you are cleaned..." She motioned to the tub, "If you would just allow us to do our jobs, we will be on our way. We will also see to it that there is food in the sitting area for you before you turn in for the evening." Belle huffed out a breath while scratching the back of her neck, rolling her shoulders once more. Shaking her head, resigned to the fact that she still wasn't going to get a moment of solitude, Belle turned her back to the woman, shifting her hair over the front of her shoulder, and she pointed to the zipper at the small of her back. The younger of the two stepped up and helped Belle step out of the dress. "No need to be shy, m'lady." She added quietly when Belle tried to cover her body out of modesty. "I will take this to the tailor for measurements. I am sure His Majesty will want our guest properly dressed by

17

morning." With that, the plump woman took the dress and vanished. "In you go, m'lady," she basically sang on her way out the door.

"Please just call me Belle... This entire situation is too foreign, and I am not formal enough for this..." The woman nodded and offered Belle a hand to guide her up the steps and down into the tub. The water was perfect, and Belle could feel all the muscles she had been fighting to keep tense start to relax. Staying in fight or flight mode was exhausting. "Even if it has to be a secret from your master, I have had enough weirdness for one day, some strange title that doesn't actually fit may be my thirteenth reason..." The woman tilted her head slightly, confused, but nodded, nonetheless.

"As you wish, Belle." Despite Belle wanting to protest, the woman literally reached into the water and began scrubbing every inch of Belle's skin until it was red and slightly raw.

The younger of the two women turned out to be named Sadie, and she spoke more candidly than Belle had expected. She told Belle that Davion was ruler of the kingdom in all but title; the Queen Mother still held the formal title. She was a stern woman who did not accept any nonsense, and that the candid nature of Belle's personality was shocking in a good way to Sadie, but that the Queen would not tolerate it. Sadie was too young to know the details of the fallout between Davion and Donovan, but just like every story, there were those who felt that Davion was the knight in shining armor, and those who believed Donovan did right by leaving with the key. Sadie refused to voice her true opinion, feeling that honest opinions may get her in trouble, and that was all Belle needed to know to gauge that Sadie would be a good friend and potential ally.

Chapter 3

Sadie helped Belle into a long, plain, black night gown as the door swung open once more. Maude, the older of the pair of women who had been assigned to Belle, came back in with a platter of food, placing it gently on the table just as she said she would. "Would you like to eat while we tend to your hair?" Belle wrinkled her brow and blinked a few times.

"Master's orders..." Sadie added, earning another frustrated huff from Belle before they watched her nod slowly.

"He and I are going to have a talk about the limitations of your duties... Safe to say that none of the royals do anything for themselves?" She asked while leveling her eyes at Sadie, "Do they bother to wipe themselves, or does that honor belong to you as well?" Both women gasped and looked nervously between each other. "It was a joke, not an honest question, ladies. Are you at least allowed to sit with me and eat? I have had an insane day, and I could use the company..." As if he had been listening, the door swung open once more, and Davion stepped into Belle's quarters. Both Sadie and Maude snapped to attention, straightening their spines and averting their eyes to the floor. Taking note of their sudden change, Belle raised a brow.

"Leave." He demanded plainly, and both women shuffled toward the door.

Mentally, Belle wanted to throw a tantrum, stomp her feet on the ground, and throw things at the towering male. She needed time to herself. From the moment that she fell into this world, things had been swirling around her non-stop, and everyone around her continued to move as if it was all normal. Belle needed to breathe; she needed to grieve.

Belle had decided a long time ago that she would never be the victim again, and because of it, her well curated, perfected mask of poise and control slid back into place. "Use your manners, princeling..." Sadie's neck snapped in Belle's direction long enough for Maude to bump into her. Davion narrowed his eyes slightly before looking at both Maude and Sadie, nodding as he murmured politeness their way. Sadie brought her hand over her heart, and she and Maude all but ran for the door, closing it behind them. "Good boy..." Belle mocked while lowering herself into a chair, snagging a grape off the platter of food. "Here... Reward yourself with some of the food that Maude brought me... Consider it a treat..." Her tone struck a chord with the prince; she could see it on his face in the way that his jaw tensed and eased, and in the way his hands flexed into fists before unclenching them. Only after he had visibly calmed himself down, Davion moved to a chair opposite Belle.

"My mother would have your tongue cut out for speaking like that... And then she would feed it to you." Belle nodded and popped the grape into her mouth, doing her best to hide her nerves behind her false bravado.

"Then I suppose it is a good thing that I am not speaking to your mother..." Shrugging, she leaned forward and grabbed another grape, popping it into her mouth before settling back into her chair once more. "So... you're a mama's boy?" Keep control, keep him on edge, she told herself while crossing one leg over the other, intentionally hiking the long night-slip up to her knees.

"I am the Queen's heir..." The words were harsh like gravel as his eyes narrowed at her.

"You are making this too easy, Davion... You would be an awful card player..." Sitting up once more, she tested the side of a bowl of soup to make sure it wasn't too hot before taking it into her hand. Slowly, almost apathetically, she leaned back in the chair, her legs folding up to her core as she tucked the black fabric between them. "So... What happened to breakfast on the terrace?" She began, avoiding eye contact with him, stirring the soup to get a feel for what she was about to eat;

thankfully, it looked like nothing but vegetables. "It's giving... desperate..." She looked up through her lashes for a moment, "As in, you must be very desperate to get between my legs to travel across this massive castle just to bother me in my room so soon after running away after I bit you..." She shifted, her honeyed eyes illuminated by the crackling fire, noting the white of his knuckles as he gripped the arms of the chair. "Don't worry... I'm not diseased."

"I have come to issue you a warning..." Davion began, and Belle nearly rolled her eyes. "If you try to run, you will be hunted. If you try anything unsavory that would not befit the presence of royalty, you will be punished."

Belle pursed her lips and narrowed her eyes. The silent itch that had started deep in her bones and had slowly started to bloom across her back flared across her flesh now as she sat across from him; almost as if something had been scratching its way to the surface, something inside of Belle had started to break free. "Yes, Prince Davion, punish me, daddy..." She rolled her eyes theatrically, savoring the way that his jaw ticked to her words; tiny victories she thought to herself. She scoffed and waved him on. "Sorry. Your threat is lacking, but please, continue..." She lifted a spoonful of vegetables with exaggerated calm, biting back a smirk when his eyebrow twitched at her command. Belle funneled her nerves into that careful motion. If she kept him on his toes, she could keep the upper hand... If she couldn't have control, she could damn well have chaos.

"I understand that you are unfamiliar with our customs, and you will be granted a certain length of leniency, but do not take advantage of the kindness that has been given to you. You are not royalty; you are to answer to royalty." He motioned to himself, a mistake.

Somewhere in her mind, a switch flipped as she snapped her eyes to Davion. "Oh..." Belle drew out the word, her lips forming a perfect O, while putting the soup back on the table. "So, when the alcohol didn't work, your next tactic was intimidation?" She stood from her seat and stepped around the table, noticing how hard Davion swallowed while she stood in front of him. Bending at the waist, she put her hands on his knees, deliberately ignoring the minute spark she felt when she touched him, before forcing them wider, lowering herself to the floor between them. "Please, your highness, take mercy on me... I am wrong and I know not what I do..." She stuck out her lower lip and pouted slightly while beginning to slide her hands up his legs. Part of Belle was determined to keep this man on edge, off guard, and unprepared for whatever she would come up with next. The other part of her, really, had no worldly reasoning for why she felt such a strong pull to him so suddenly. Sure. He looked like Donovan. And sure, they had slept together plenty of times... But this wasn't Donovan, and the logical side of Belle's mind already knew that. The illogical didn't seem to care. That itch at the core of her being stopped, and something new was crawling out. Some unknown calm was blanketing Belle as her actions furthered her agenda to control the situation one way or another.

Belle began to scoff and push off his legs to stand, but before she could, the black smoke vines yanked the table aside, damn near throwing it into the fire. The tray of food that covered it flew across the room, the fire hissing when the soup crashed into it. Davion lunged with lightning quickness, knocking Belle onto her back and pinning her beneath him. He ripped her hands from her sides and slammed them over her head, trapping them with one hand as his other clamped around her throat, tight enough to part her lips and steal her breath. He leaned down, his nose nearly brushing hers, his voice a dangerous growl. "Stop. Talking." With each word, he squeezed tighter. Belle's eyes burned. Her lips parted again, this time with a sharp gasp, and to her horror, a moan slipped free.

Davion froze for half a second, the sound released from her plump lips like a trigger. His pupils dilated like a predator catching scent. Then his grip shifted, ruthless, but less certain, and he yanked the black fabric of her nightgown upward, exposing her legs as he straddled her, knee pressing between her thighs.

Belle's body reacted before her brain did, before logic had any chance to catch up. Her breath came faster. Her limbs trembled, not with fear, but with something else. Something unfamiliar. Something wrong, and hot. What the hell was happening to her? She twisted beneath him, trying to push him off, but the vines of smoke wrapped around her ankles like

22

shackles, pinning her to the floor. They slithered up her thighs, containing, controlling, spreading her open like a flower under moonlight. This was power. It was meant to scare her. He wanted her to beg. And gods help her; she wanted to fight; she wanted to claw her way free and leave him bleeding.

However her body didn't want to listen. "Open," Davion ordered, holding two fingers in front of her lips. His voice had dropped—rougher now, almost strained.

Belle shook her head, jaw tight, but her lips parted. Not from obedience. From something deeper.

Feed.

The word wasn't Belle's. It wasn't even a thought. It was instinct. A whisper from beneath her skin, hungry, ancient, and undeniable.

Davion slid his fingers into her mouth, not gentle, not caring, and Belle tasted power, raw and bitter, laced with heat. It pulsed on her tongue like static, and something in her snapped awake. Her cheeks flushed. Her blood felt molten, and her breath quickened.

His fingers left her mouth, and before she could process it, they were trailing lower, gliding with terrifying precision. Her back arched involuntarily, her thighs twitching. Every nerve in her body lit up. No. No. This isn't happening... But it was. Her hips lifted to meet his hand. Her eyes fluttered shut against her will. Her breath stuttered, half a gasp, half a growl. She didn't understand it. She didn't want it. But something inside of her yearned for it.

He knew what he was doing. She could feel it in every calculated curl of his fingers, every firm circle over her clit, every press into the exact place that made her hips jerk. He touched her like a man used to control, and for the first time, control was slipping right through his fingers.

Belle's lips parted again. A moan spilled out.

Davion inhaled sharply, his eyes going nearly black. He clenched his jaw, muscles twitching. His rhythm was halted by the unfamiliar flash that ripped through him. "Good girl..." he mocked, after taking a sharp breath, shaking his head. His voice low and too steady to be real. She glared at him, hate blooming in her chest, but her body betrayed her again, arching toward him, chasing the sensation, the pressure, the heat.

"You're soaking my fingers, Belle," he hissed. "All that fire in your mouth and look at you now." She whimpered. It wasn't weakness, it was rage. Confusion. Something primal was rising in her belly and making her shake. "Come for me." He leaned his head down and his lips brushed her ear. "Do it."

Her body obeyed before her mind caught up. The orgasm slammed into her like a freight train, robbing her breath and pulling the moan from her throat in a wild, broken sound. Her back arched. Her vision blurred. And somewhere in the middle of it, Belle felt something pull. Not from her, but into her. Like heat siphoning off him, feeding her, fueling her.

Davion swore under his breath. His vines fell away like they'd burned themselves out, and he shoved himself to his feet, stumbling slightly as he adjusted himself. His face was flushed. His chest heaved. Belle sat up slowly, fury bubbling in her blood now that her head was beginning to clear. Her mouth opened to speak, but he was already crouching again. He shoved two fingers back into her mouth, the same ones soaked with her release. "Stop. Talking." His tone had shifted, low, dangerous, but not victorious. There was something haunted in it. He wiped his fingers across her bottom lip, then licked them clean as he stood.

"Remember this," he said, barely looking at her, "the next time you mouth off." Then, as if nothing had happened at all, he turned and walked to the door. Closing it softly behind him. Davion paused at the door as it latched, his pulse roaring in his head like the ocean in the middle of a storm. He stared blankly down at the floor, forcing himself to take a steadying breath, and fighting every urge in his body to go back into Belle's room and finish what he just started.

Belle collapsed onto her back, staring up at the ceiling like it might have answers. Her pulse thundered in her ears. Her skin still tingled. Her breath was shallow, ragged.

"What the fuck," she whispered, and for once, she had nothing clever to add.

Belle didn't bother with blankets or pillows when she finally fell onto the bed. She couldn't move. Her body felt used, her skin still humming with something she didn't understand, like an aftershock from a spell she hadn't cast. It was the first moment of stillness since everything exploded. A sliver of silence between one world ending and the next beginning. She should be planning an escape. Plotting revenge. Something. Anything. But all she could do was lie there, legs dangling over the side of the bed, staring at nothing as the weight of the day, of him, settled into her bones.

Her thoughts didn't spiral. They stormed. They raged and they twisted, reviewing and reliving her entire day. Every thought, every twist, and every turn mentally swirled around Belle. Each pain and every ache thrummed heavily in her mind and on her body. And eventually, she drowned in her mental storm enough to drift to sleep.

Belle didn't dream; she didn't stir at all in her sleep, not until she heard the door open and the cheerful voice of Maude singing morning praises. Belle grunted and rolled on the bed, taking the blanket with her to hide from daylight as Maude threw open the tall curtains at the windows of the room. "No ma'am, not today. You are having breakfast with Prince Davion. The Queen has heard of your arrival; from what whisperings that we have heard, and she will be joining as well. Which puts us in a bit of a time crunch, as you appear to need some extra care."

"Tell the Queen she can eat shit," Belle grumbled from beneath the blankets, and Maude gasped like she had just witnessed a public execution.

She stormed across the room and ripped the blankets right off, pointing a finger in her face, "You will have more respect for the Queen, if not for your own sake, then for ours. Now get out of this bed at once." Belle recoiled slightly and blinked a few times before nodding. When Maude nodded in return and stepped back, she was straightening the length of the apron that covered her long skirt; some sort of symbolism of having her feathers ruffled was all Belle could assume.

"So, I'm not even allowed a minute to process the fact that I fell, yes, literally fell into another world, discovered that magic is real, and like... super common here, I guess? I watched my best friend maybe die..." Saying the words out loud choked Belle for a second. She straightened her spine, "And then got manhandled by the crown prince?" She trailed off, first, realizing that she was processing out loud, secondly, catching the glance from both women, to herself, and then back to each

25

other. "Hmm... What is it? What's that?" Belle wagged a finger between the two of them.

"Nothing, m'lady, we haven't the time." Sadie piped up with a little nod before draping some sort of undergarment over Belle's head, quickly followed by a layer of deep blue from Maude.

When the women were done fussing over Belle, her hair had been half braided, leaving a few select curls loose here and there, and the dress they had literally laced her into was something out of a fairytale. The deep blue layer served as the base, covered by another layer in a silken fabric cut differently than the underlayer, making the deep blue color more of an accent. To top it off, they strapped Belle into a corset, pulling the damned thing so tight she was sure she heard and felt a rib pop. "The seamstress requests that we leave all of these with you for your potentially prolonged stay. I will see to it that they are properly arranged in your wardrobe. Sadie will take you down to the terrace." Maude shooed both Sadie and Belle toward the door.

No sooner did the pair take four steps away from the door, than Belle leaned in toward Sadie, "So... What am I walking into? What was that glance between the two of you before getting me dressed?" Sadie shook her head and brought a single finger to her lips while stepping closer to Belle as they walked.

"Her Royal Highness will not appreciate your unique level of impertinence. I dare say you should keep it to a minimum if possible. Follow the Prince's lead; he understands you have not had the same years of etiquette training as he and Princess Khandra, his sister, have had." She bit her bottom lip before looking around, ensuring that they were alone. "As for your comments on the prince's dealings. He is stern in his own way. He has been so focused on the keys and finding Donovan that he hasn't been with anyone since Donovan left. He likely wishes to claim you and wash Donovan's scent from you if there is one..." She hesitated, "If you two had..." Belle nodded and rolled her eyes. But something in her gut twisted. The way Davion touched her last night wasn't just possession. It was desperation. And worse, something in Belle had responded.

"So, it's a pissing match..." Sadie squinted, "A challenge for them to see whose dick is bigger?" Sadie shrugged, "A way for them to assert their dominance over a female to 'claim them' as if they were an owned piece of property." Sadie's eyes shifted around, processing Belle's words before she nodded in affirmation.

"Your speech is so funny." Sadie shook her head and smiled before opening the tall glass doors that took them to a large stone patio. The perimeter had an outer rim of stone, carved carefully to form what could be a fence, but the interior was lined with a thin row of green bushes. In the center of the patio was a round metal table with three chairs, and three places set. The table was covered in all kinds of colorful fruit, small bowls of meats, eggs, and various sizes and shapes of bread. "Oh... When the Queen arrives, make sure you stand and curtsy. If you don't, she'll have someone whip your ankles while she sits back and smiles."

"I will take it from here, Sadie. You are dismissed..." A low voice came from behind them; Belle turned and lofted a brow before nodding toward Sadie while staring Davion directly in his eyes. "Thank you..." he added, somewhat begrudgingly, before intentionally looking away from Belle as she started to smile. "Sadie is correct, though. My mother will not tolerate your specific style of attitude as I so graciously have." He extended a hand toward one of the three seats and he stepped behind it, allowing Belle to sit before scooting her closer to the table.

"Don't cuss at the Queen... Got it..." Belle exhaled before fidgeting with the layers of skirt that fell all around her, taking a settling breath while looking out past the patio at the elaborate steps which led down to what looked like a vast garden, and beyond it a massive forest. "Do women not wear pants in your kingdom?" She motioned at the dress as Davion sat next to her.

"They can, and they do." He folded his hands in his lap before allowing his eyes to wander, taking in the sight of Belle from head to toe. "I just wanted to see you in my colors..." Belle nodded, noting the possessive tone that he carried when he said *my*.

Chapter 4

"This is our intruder…" A woman's voice came from the doorway, and both Davion and Belle shot up from their seats, turning to face her. The woman who walked toward them had sharp features; even her cheekbones seemed like they had a point to them, with the most stunning salt and pepper colored hair pulled back into an ornate updo that accentuated the crown at the top of her head. Her dress was a similar style to Belle's, but all layers of grey and black. The jewelry that she wore had the same blue that Davion had deemed his color.

Belle did her best to curtsy despite the initial reaction of wanting to mouth off to the woman for how she greeted Belle. Davion greeted his mother with a small bow, followed by kissing both of her cheeks and helping her into her seat the way that he had with Belle moments before. "She's prettier than the last whore that you had me sit through breakfast with… Though likely just as stupid…" Belle looked to Davion, who shook his head slightly. Belle balled her hands into her fists in her lap, nails biting at the palms of her hands. "Let us eat. One of you can explain the happenings that I seem to have missed out on." No sooner had the words left her mouth than three small men appeared from nowhere. They filled the plates in front of everyone and vanished again. Fucking royalty also meant you couldn't plate your own food? Belle thought to herself. "Well… One of you, speak." Queen Martine demanded while waving a fork before stabbing it into something on her plate.

It was Belle who beat Davion to the punch, "I fell through a portal, thanks to a key, with your other son, Donovan, whom Davion left in a field to die. I have been given very little information on where I am, what is going on, or apparently, what I am, and according to your only living son here, I am not entirely human, or I would not have made it through the portal. And then last night..." Davion cleared his throat, cutting Belle off with a sharp glare. She met his eyes and lofted a brow, issuing a silent challenge.

"What our guest means to say..." Davion cut in before Belle could continue to push her Earthen way. "She and Donovan were brought back to our realm with the help of the key that he stole; the full details of how that happened have not been discussed with Belle yet. She was unaware of what the key was, or even what Donovan was, when she was brought here; nor did Donovan ever tell her he could tell she had magic. I will be taking her to the Magus Tower directly after breakfast for further examination." Belle lofted a brow; this was news to her. Mimicking the Queen's movements with the silverware, she tried to seem more proper than she really was. "I have already sent scouts to recover Donovan's body so that we can give it to one of the Mancer's to find the key that he returned with. During her time here, Belle is being tended to by Sadie and Maude; they will see to it that she falls in line. If not, I will deal with her." Davion gave Belle a knowing look, certainly referring to her treatment last night.

"So why is she here?" The Queen asked indifferently between bites.

"She was uninjured, and we are not savages." Davion shrugged, "If she was in fact in league with Donovan, there may be information about his plan that we are able to find. We should see if she could be useful either in her knowledge or the magic in her blood." Belle sat quietly, looking between the two as they continued to have a conversation as if she weren't right there. Any other day, any other situation, Belle would have already reached across the table and slapped the taste out of the woman's mouth for being such a bitch; however, she had been warned.

"She belongs in the dungeon, not in a room with ladies and custom gowns. If she is to be your plaything, speak it outright, fool." The Queen crossed her knife under the fork across her plate while shaking her head as if she were suddenly disgusted by her food. "She would make a great plaything, don't you think, Davion?"

Belle dropped the fork and knife onto the plate with a clatter, "Hi, yes, hello. I am sitting right here." She huffed out a breath, warning be damned. If the Queen decided to kill her for speaking her mind, so be it. It wasn't exactly like Belle was plush with family and friends back home... "I am no one's 'plaything', whatever that means in your world." There had been a time, years and years ago, that Belle was a meek, timid, quiet girl, and she served only the people who used and abused her. She had vowed never again, even if it hurt.

She placed her hands on the edge of the table before continuing, "I am not some sort of whore, nor am I stupid. If you would so politely get off your high horse, you may recognize that the way you speak about people, especially in their presence, is abhorrent; and speaks volumes about your own character." Belle glared a hole straight through the Queen's grey eyes as she tightened the grip on the table, almost certain that she was signing her own death warrant. "I did not ask to come here, or to be involved in this shit in any way, shape or fo-" A black tendril, darker and more solid than Davion's shot across the table, slapping Belle in the mouth with enough force to split her lip, stopping her in her tracks. She was only momentarily phased before she stood fast enough to topple the metal chair that she had been sitting in. "You bi-" Davion's black smoke enveloped Belle entirely as he sprang to his feet, wrapping tightly around her body, constricting her movement, her airflow, everything.

When it faded, Belle had just enough time to recognize the familiar stone room and see Davion storming toward her before slamming her back against the wall. His hand was tight around her throat. "Were you not warned?" He roared in her face, eyes almost black as night. "The Queen does as she pleases, as is her right! You are nothing... Nothing to her! Do you hear me?" His hand tightened and Belle's vision started to blur. When her eyes started to roll and her body began to fall limp, he released his grip and smacked her across the face, "You do not get to faint on me right now."

With her bleeding lip running fresh again, Belle spat the blood in Davion's face before bringing her left fist across his cheek as hard as she could. "I will not be treated like I am a fucking object, Davion." She all but hissed when he stepped back and grabbed his cheek, "And I will not be talked to like garbage, especially by strangers." Belle knew herself well enough to know that if she survived the night, she would likely crumble and cry; she could feel the knot building in her throat even now. She needed to be strong; she refused to back down, she couldn't. Therapy could only treat so much trauma; a thousand images threatened to flash, a thousand painful memories with them.

Davion narrowed his eyes at her now, the smoke tendrils creeping along the ground toward Belle as he slowly approached, fire in his eyes. He trailed his tongue across his lips where her blood had landed. She held her hands up defensively, doing her best not to shake as fear started to overtake her courage. "Back... Off..." She tried to come across as threatening, but when Davion stopped in his tracks, Belle tilted her head to the side and watched as he took not one, but two steps back.

"How did you do that?" He asked, voice still full of fury, tensing his muscles, willing his body forward, but it wouldn't move.

"Do what?" She watched as he took another step back. She had told him to back off, and here he was, very slowly taking steps backward. "Kneel..."

He dropped. His eyes snapped to her, wide, stunned. "Succubus." The word escaped like a curse. He blinked once, "Succubus," he said again, this time with weight. "You're a fucking succubus... Last night... There was something about last night that was beyond out of character for me. And I just ingested your blood." He shook his head slowly. "We have to get you to the mages now, Belle." The anger had faded from his tone, and he looked up at her, almost as if he was pleading. "Please release me so that I can take you." The gentleness that came across in his voice now was something she hadn't heard before; it shook her to her core just enough to make her fully believe him.

"I... How?" She fumbled with her words. "I release you." There was a confused tone in her voice as she wrinkled her brow, but no sooner did the words come out of her mouth

31

than Davion stood. He was on her in a flash, grabbing her wrist and pulling her into the dark smoke with him.

Stepping out on the other side, they were in a round stone room, full of bottles. Bottles lined shelves, covering bookcases, backs of desks, even bottles melted into the wax from the candles that illuminated the room. Between the bottles were books of all shapes and sizes, and one large part of the wall was covered in a custom shelf meant to hold dozens and dozens of scrolls. Letting go of her wrist, Davion waved a dismissive hand as the six mages in their long white robes bowed to him. "Test her. Do it now." He nudged Belle forward, keeping a hand at the small of her back. "Will you behave?" He asked while leaning into her neck.

"Is this something that I need to behave for?" She turned toward him, their lips dangerously close. Davion backed away, standing straight with a little nod. "Is it going to hurt?" Belle asked while cocking a brow as three of the mages pulled a thick wooden chair toward the center of the room.

"Like seven hells..." Davion muttered while continuing to nudge Belle toward the chair. As she sat, the mages wrapped thick leather straps at her wrists, waist, thighs, and ankles; her eyes shot to Davion in panic. "It's just for the test." He was doing his best to keep his tone neutral, but somewhere inside, he was hating that they were going to have to do this. Hating what they were going to find, and what it could mean for anyone in the room. If she truly was a succubus and the Queen heard about it, she would surely have Belle banished to the Waste, and for some reason Davion couldn't put his finger on, he wasn't ready to lose her yet... Maybe it was just the succubus magic, or maybe underneath his cold exterior, he did have a heart.

One of the men in their long robes stepped to Belle, pricking her finger before taking the small, single bead of blood into a glass vial. Yet another jar for this room's extensive collection, Belle thought to herself. A second started toward Belle with a small glass vial of sickly-looking green liquid. Belle already started to recoil, trying to push herself back into the chair as if she could push herself through it. "Give it here." Davion shook his head and held out his hand. The mage handed over the vial and gave a little bow before backing up.

32

"This will not feel good, princess... But I will be right here as you suffer..." Belle shook her head before turning away from Davion. He grunted, displeased by her reaction. "Open." He demanded, narrowing his dark eyes slightly. Belle continued to shake her head, reminiscent of the night before. "I said... Open..." He repeated, more gravel in his voice while he trailed his thumb at the corner of her lips. With a huffed exhale, Belle locked eyes with Davion and tilted her head back, opening her mouth wide and sticking her tongue out. His jaw ticked, and he shook his head slightly, "Good girl..." He muttered before pouring the liquid into her mouth, clamping his hand down over her lips; he knew what was to follow.

Belle's eyes went wide, and she attempted to shake her head, to get Davion off of her, but the bitter, sour taste had her cringing and recoiling; there was nothing appealing about the liquid as it passed from her mouth when she swallowed. Before the rancid taste could fade, her entire body started to burn from the inside out. It started low in her stomach before blooming up into her chest, down to her thighs, slowly consuming her. She closed her eyes tightly, gritting her teeth to keep from screaming.

Davion stepped back and handed the vial to one of the mages, folding his arms over his chest, his jaw ticking as he watched Belle be put through this unique form of torture. His index finger tapped impatiently on his arm, hoping it would be quick. Hoping it would be quiet. Belle threw her head back and let out an ear-piercing scream, her honey brown eyes glowing momentarily before going stark white, and then her body went limp in the chair. They all welcomed the silence after the volume and pitch that Belle had reached, but Davion's eyes were locked on Belle.

The room was cold. Silent. The six mages were arranged in a circle, as still as statues. They knew that forcing power to the forefront could be dangerous, especially when the person in question was unconscious. Over the years, it became the easiest way to identify the powers that people carried; and the once torturous process that took days could now be done in a matter of hours with the mages refining the concoction over and over again.

Belle's breathing hitched. Her back arched hard against the chair. "She cannot be waking," one of the mages murmured, worry edging his voice.

"She isn't," another mage all but whispered, his gaze transfixed. "She's... dreaming." Belle's mind floated between planes, but something inside her stirred. Not her conscious self, but something different. Something older. The clawing feeling that she had felt since she fell into this place, that itch at the center of her spine scratching for its own freedom; it had been her magic all along. And it didn't bloom, it blazed like a fire crawling through the forest, slow and hungry, oh so hungry.

The mages felt it. One by one, their breathing changed. The air grew thick. Eyes that were once sharp with focus drifted to Belle, to her lips, to the way she writhed in the chair as if she knew they were watching.

In her mind, Belle could feel them; feel the way their bodies craved hers. She could see herself reflected in their desires, the way that they all began to undress her with their eyes; images flashing through her mind from theirs. In this moment, she had become every fantasy they've never dared whisper aloud. The youngest mage stumbled forward. Just a step. Then another. The others didn't stop him, they couldn't stop him, they were all frozen in place, slowly losing a battle to desire. His hand trembled as he reached for her wrist, aiming to unbind her.

The moment his finger brushed Belle's arm, he was frozen as her power surged. A deep thrum of satisfaction ripped through them both. He wanted her, the contact feeling like the only thing he could ever crave. The mage shifted slightly, wrapping his whole hand around Belle's wrist, yearning for more contact, more sensation. It washed over him in waves, powerful, sensual waves. Belle's eyes slowly opened, glowing golden while still in the dream state, as the mage slowly fell limp on the ground next to them. Belle couldn't contain it; she exhaled a prolonged moan, her glowing eyes locking onto Davion, while she pulled roughly at the bindings. All she could see was him, his strength, his power, his desire for her.

Despite the waves crashing against him, Davion remained a rock in the middle of a turbulent ocean. Arms folded over his chest, expression unreadable. "This stays here," he growled, only shifting his eyes to the elder mage on his left before refocusing his attention on Belle. "No one can know, or they will deal with me. Are we understood?" The elder mage nodded and pulled a small blade from his robes while watching the remaining mages tend to the fallen mage on the ground.

Belle shifted in her seat, not so much pulling at the restraints as she was trying to ease her nerves that felt like they were on fire. "He's still breathing." One mage muttered, horrified. Belle blinked a few times, the burning desire fading quickly as she breathed sharp, ragged breaths.

"Then why does it feel like I've killed him?" She asked while leaning to the side, still bound to the chair. While she tried to get a better look at him, panic rising in her tone as she fought with the binds to see the body on the ground.

Davion cautiously closed the distance between them. He hesitated momentarily, having seen exactly what the power that Belle had within her could do. Despite the quiet fear that trickled in his mind, Davion unlatched the leather bands and held his hand out to her, helping her back to her feet as all but one of the mages gathered around their fallen brethren. The elder mage turned his attention to Davion, and instinctively he pulled Belle into his arms, as if protecting her from the man.

"Who was her mother?" The eldest mage hissed while approaching them with the first small vial with Belle's blood in it in his hands, holding it up toward them as if they could see the answer in the vial like the mage could.

"Irrelevant," Davion stated plainly, narrowing his eyes.

"Not at all." The mages worked at the youngest, bringing him potions to revitalize him. "If this is right," He guided them toward the other side of the room to speak more plainly. "...and my magic is never wrong," The mage added with a faint nod, "her blood is old, ancient, forgotten to this world as long ago as the battle of the keys had begun." Davion took a small glance at Belle before looking back at the eldest mage, waiting for him to elaborate, "Her line was one of the first to go through the portals to other realms. They were chosen. They were trusted among the rulers of all the kingdoms at the time. Power was promised to them upon their return from another realm." He shook his head and looked to Belle, "They never did return." Belle shifted awkwardly, finding herself leaning

35

into Davion while this odd man stared her down. "If her magic line has been dormant in another realm this entire time... If I didn't know any better... I would say that the magic in her blood has been strengthening this entire time." His eyes seemed to cross a little as he looked back to the vial, holding it up to the candlelight.

"There is no magic where I'm from..." Belle added quietly, and the mage nodded, as if her quiet admission was all of the confirmation that he needed.

"Do I need to repeat myself about your silence?" Davion's voice lowered, entering threatening territory while he stared down the elder mage. Only with half a thought, he pulled Belle closer to himself.

"Give me your tongues..." The elder mage began before tossing the bloodied vial into the fire, disposing of the evidence of Belle's bloodlines return. Turning toward the rest of the mages, he drew a small blade from within the sleeve of his robe. One by one, they bared their tongues, letting him carve a rune. They each accepted with no hesitation. Even the youngest, barely conscious, was marked. The elder mage turned the blade on himself, carving the same rune while looking at Belle and Davion; a small sign of the loyalty that this man had to the Prince, not the Queen.

As the rune was laid onto each of their tongues, Belle grabbed Davion's arm, looking up to him, puzzled. "If they are questioned about this... If they try to speak about this... at all, in any form... They will die a painful death." He whispered to her, while making a meticulous mental note of which mages were present, his chest quietly rising in pride that they had chosen loyalty to him, and not blindly to the crown.

Chapter 5

Once the mages had sworn their silence, Davion took Belle by the wrist, and in a rush of shadow, they vanished. They reappeared in Belle's chambers, light spilling over them. Davion was already behind her, nudging her forward as his fingers worked quickly at the corset ties. Belle stretched her arms overhead, spine arching as the garment loosened. He muttered under his breath, fighting with the layers he himself had insisted on. At the time, it seemed appropriate. Now, he cursed every button and ribbon. "Don't fight me on this. Just get in the bath," he said, nodding toward the tub.

Belle raised an eyebrow, tilting her head, but didn't move. Only as she watched as he began to remove his clothes did it fully register that she was standing naked in front of him. "Is this a sex thing?" She asked as she stepped into the tub, lowering herself into the water with a calming sigh. He shook his head while stepping out of his pants.

"Look at me, Belle." As if she wasn't already staring. He reached over to her, in the tub, and grabbed her chin gently, forcing her to look at him. "I will give you answers. Everything you seek. But for both of our safety, I need you naked... And I need you close. I will not destroy you. Not yet." There was a softness in his tone that twisted her confusion into something more primal. Her lips parted, but no words came.

He climbed into the tub and took up the washcloth, moving behind her. With careful fingers, he brushed her hair off her neck and began to run the cloth over her shoulders. Her power, whatever she had awakened, was tearing him apart from the inside. All he could think about was bending her over

37

the edge of the tub. Making her moan. Hearing her moan his name. Surely being naked was not the smartest move, but he needed his hands on her, and this gave him a valid excuse.

Davion was surprised to see that she wasn't fighting him. He was under the assumption that she was in some form of shock from what she had unleashed in the mage's tower. Despite the raw power she exuded, Davion was at war with himself. Every instinct screamed to take, to claim, but something quieter held him back. He knew she had been through a lot, and that a little tenderness could go a long way; she didn't need dominance right now. She needed softness. Restraint. And gods help him, he would give it to her... even as it tore at every thread of his control. She had come so close to killing that poor boy in the tower, and Davion knew that Belle didn't know the consequences that killing carried.

"Your kind have been hunted for centuries," Davion said as he laced their fingers together, guiding her to turn and offering her arm to the water. His gaze stayed on her skin, his touch deliberate, yet he felt the weight of her stare, ravenous and unrelenting, as if she was already craving more of that power she'd barely begun to taste. "You're not necessarily stronger than the rest of us," he continued, voice low. "But the ability to persuade... to seduce... has toppled kingdoms. Chawbig. Tilahia. Rombor. All fell at the hands of incubi and succubi, until they were forced back into the Waste. Entire kingdoms purged and rebuilt from nearly nothing." Davion took a deep breath, steadying himself, "None of history really writes it as a coordinated effort... The people who tore the kingdoms to shreds were just power hungry... They didn't just want a seat at the table; they wanted the crown."

He paused, switching to her other arm. "The Waste sits at the southern edge of the Wildelands. There's a wall, built to cage succubi and incubi behind it. The guards stationed there are trained, torturously so, to resist your kind's influence." He guided a finger along her shoulders, bringing goosebumps to his own flesh just touching her. The power that had flooded the room still pulled through him, and Davion had to fight it to keep his mind straight. "People from every kingdom send their best trained youth to The Waste, and then they are trained all over again." He shook his head slightly, "I would hate to come up against one of them."

Davion moved the cloth to her neck, trailing it slowly downward. "If any of you cross that wall... the penalty is death. No questions. No mercy." Belle's body stiffened. She nodded, slow and dazed. "That's why my mother can't know."

"Because she will kill me." Belle moved easily under Davion's gentle command, turning so he could lower her hair into the water. When she rose again, he leaned close, unable to resist, and took a slow, deep breath. His hand slid from her shoulder to her jaw, his thumb grazing her lower lip. She smelled like the edge of a forest. Earthy. Wild. Blooming. Like spring wrapped in something far more dangerous.

"I don't want you to stop..." Her voice was barely a whisper. "But you only want me because I'm some kind of sex creature." She licked the tip of his thumb as it passed her mouth, pressing her bare body against his. "Torturing you is going to be glorious."

In one smooth motion, he spun her forward. Belle caught herself on the edge of the tub just as Davion pressed the length of his cock against her slit. "And the punishment I shall inflict for such torture," he growled into her ear, "will be exquisite." His hand slid around her throat, squeezing. Tight enough to control. Soft enough not to break. "You are a danger to me, Belle."

With a curse under his breath, he forced himself away. He retreated to the far side of the tub, his breath ragged, his eyes still locked on her.

Belle turned slowly, deliberately. She mirrored his pose, arms resting on the edges of the tub like a queen already certain of her victory. "I can see why my kind are such a threat to you." She smirked and licked her bottom lip.

"Her kind?" The voice rang like a bell from the doorway. A tall woman with short black hair strolled in, hands folded primly at her waist.

"Khandra..." Davion muttered, already exasperated.

"Please, don't stop on my account. I do enjoy a good show." Her heels clicked across the stone as she came to lean a hip on the tub, eyes bright with mischief. Belle crossed her arms over her bare chest, but Khandra only smiled wider.

39

"Come now, Belle. We're both women. Same parts. I'll show you mine sometime." She tugged at the laces of her corset with deliberate flair. "Though, I'm far more curious what you meant by 'my kind'..." She bent slightly, propping her elbows on the tub's edge and resting her chin in her hands, studying Belle like a cat with a trapped bird.

"Go away, Khandra. This doesn't concern you," Davion growled.

"On the contrary, dear brother." Her eyes sparkled. "I return from a little holiday, and what do I hear? Whispers of Donovan's return, a murder, and a mysterious beauty who has captured the attention of my last living sibling." She clutched her chest in mock delight. "I'm simply enthralled. I'm dying to meet my soon-to-be sister."

Belle opened her mouth to object, but Khandra waved her off. "Yes, yes, you just met. Blah blah blah. But look at him." She nodded toward Davion. "Those puppy dog eyes? Haven't seen them in centuries. And here I find the two of you naked, flushed, and very clearly aroused." She sniffed the air theatrically. "I could smell it from the bedroom."

Khandra tilted her head. "Almost as if she were a..."

Belle's jaw twitched.
Davion stood.

"Oh..." Khandra smiled like a knife. She made a soft tsking sound. "Very much like a bitch in heat, then." She flicked a lazy finger toward Davion's obvious state of arousal. "Don't worry, dear brother. Your secret's safe with me. Anything to spite our mother. Perhaps you'll even share." She winked at Belle. "I expect a private dinner this evening. Just us three. No prying ears. You remember the way, Davion. Clothing optional, of course." With a lilting laugh, she waved a hand and sauntered out. "Breed her well, sweet prince. Your throne will require an heir."

Silence.

Davion climbed out of the tub with a splash, grabbed a towel, and scrubbed both hands over his face and into his hair. "Absolute bag of wind, that one."

40

"Courtland." A small man appeared, barely reaching Belle's shoulder, with a folded pile of clothes in his arms. "Fetch the dagger as well." Courtland nodded, handed over the clothing, and vanished again.

"Out," Davion told Belle. "Khandra doesn't mean dinner. She means now. Everything with her is now. Spoiled brat." Belle sank a little deeper into the water, cutting her eyes at him. "Please..." he muttered under his breath.

Courtland returned with a small, sheathed blade. Davion took it. The man vanished again.

"I will never get used to this place," Belle muttered, climbing out of the bath. Even while dressing, she could feel Davion's gaze on her. Watching how she moved. Studying her like a puzzle he was desperate to solve.

Once she had finished doing her best to reassemble the morning's outfit, she turned to him and shrugged slightly, as if asking if it would do.

He mirrored her shrug, then held out the blade. "Until you learn to control what you are, you'll need protection. Your sharp tongue cuts deep, but it won't always be enough." Davion hooked the silver chain around her waist, sliding the blade to her hip.

"Careful, princeling. You might start looking like you have a heart."

"Just protecting what's mine." He pulled her closer, hands on her hips. She rested a hand on his chest, a subtle barrier. Probably more for her than him.

Her brow twitched... That word... It sounded too final, too binding. "What, is this some kind of weird magical creature thing? If I let you fuck me, I'll suddenly be all goo-goo eyed over you?" She scoffed. "As if you own me."

"Fae, Belle. We all have fae blood. Not magical creatures. We're not manticores or dragons."
He watched her expression shift. "I believe your world calls us fairies. Elves. That sort of thing."

She opened her mouth to respond. He didn't let her. "And," he added, stepping in close and pinning her with his gaze, "...when I fuck you, and I will, you'll never want another." He pressed her back against the armoire. "Don't forget, Belle. I made you fall apart on my fingers alone. Imagine what else I

41

could do." He leaned closer, voice dropping lower. "Never. Another."

Then he stepped back, cool and composed once again. "Now. To appease the brat princess." He tapped her cheek lightly; more threat than affection.

Chapter 6

They walked arm-in-arm to the tower that had been entirely reserved for Khandra. The walls were decorated with paintings and tapestries, as if trying to hide the masonry beneath them. Even the cold stone floor had carpet laid along its length to soften it.

They stepped into Khandra's chamber just as a tall, broad-shouldered man slipped past them, shirt half-tucked, boots in hand. He gave a haphazard bow in Belle's direction before disappearing into the hall.

Khandra lounged on a chaise, a half-empty glass of something sparkling in her hand, hair slightly mussed but her smirk entirely in place. "Forgive the mess," she purred, eyes dragging over Belle as if she was cataloging her. "I was just so worked up after seeing you two earlier..." Khandra straightened the layers of her skirts before smiling brightly at Belle, "Oh, good, you understood that I meant now... Though I hadn't expected you so soon..." Her gaze slid to Davion, "Losing your touch, brother..." She poked at him before motioning for them to sit. "Or..." She shifted, looking to Belle, "Or maybe she is just that amazing..."

"Khandra is insatiable..." Davion muttered while waiting for Belle to take a seat before lowering himself onto the couch beside her. "You would think that she was a succubus with how she runs through the staff..."

"There could still be a chance," Khandra all but sang lightly, "We all know how our bitch of a mother talks about our father..." She spoke so dismissively of the Queen that it almost gave Belle hope for this strange woman. "Anyway. We are not

43

here about me..." She looked around the room at the various servants scurrying around, "Go on." She flicked her fingers at the bustle of attendants. Some vanished as swiftly as Courtland had for Davion; others shut doors behind them, but they all quickly made their exit.

Khandra sat up, leaning toward Belle, "My, my, my, you've barely been here two days, and you've already been assaulted." She shook her head and waved a hand toward Belle in the same fashion that Davion would use to release the tendrils of smoke. A chill swept over Belle, sinking into the split in her lip. It traveled through her body, unknotting tense muscles until she nearly melted into the cushions.

"I have the power of time... Selectively..." Khandra offered with a shrug. "Such as healing wounds by rewinding an injury. Or opening old ones if I must." Khandra cringed slightly at the thought before sitting back in the chaise, brushing an errant hair from her face. "Now, from what Sadie says, you are a spitfire. Not common here, where women are to be seen, not heard." She let out a light laugh. "That's why I have so much room in the castle. Mother thinks that by showering me with trinkets, she keeps me busy; far from her plans for dear Davion." Belle opened her mouth to speak, but Khandra carried on. "Sadie says you even mouthed off to the Queen... Hence the..." She motioned at her own lip instead of voicing it. "You're lucky that Davion had enough of a heart to spare you from the wrath that was surely to follow..."

"Khandra. Enough." Davion's voice cracked like a whip. "What is your price for silence on the matter of her blood?" He asked while gesturing toward Belle.

Her dark eyes locked on Davion's, and a slow, devious smile curled at her lips. "Out with it, you witch." He demanded.

"I want her for a night when she comes into her power..." Khandra crossed her legs, shifting her hips slightly.

Belle's temper snapped. "What the fuck is with you people? Your mother calls me his plaything, now you're treating me like property" Belle burst out while throwing her hands up in frustration as she stood, beginning to pace. "Some spoiled fucking nymphomaniac princess wanting me to fuck her because of something in my blood, that I don't even know,

44

understand, or want! Fuck that!" Belle flicked her hair over her shoulder before pointing an accusatory finger at Khandra, "You want that so badly. Go to the Waste. Have a blast."

"Oh, I have." Khandra rose, closing the space between them. "But you... You're exotic. A rarity. A delicacy." She caught Belle's hands for the briefest moment.

Belle slapped her before she could think twice. "So go fuck a manticore." Davion was on his feet now, too, jaw tight.

"Please," Khandra said, her tone cooling, like a switch had been flipped. "Sit down. Both of you. The last thing we need is a ruckus and guards barging in while we toss around the word succubus." She waited until Belle and Davion retook their seats. "I apologize; I only wanted to see the fire that Sadie spoke so highly of. I have no interest in taking you from my brother. My silence is free, as always. But I would like to hear about your world, Belle. Our libraries tell us only so much. I'd hoped to visit, but I hear the key has vanished again..."

"Gods alive, Khandra. I thought there was some unseen magic happening here, and I was going to have to restrain you and remove her." Davion took a loud, deep breath.

The sudden talk of the keys was a sobering thought to Belle. She silently berated herself for not having thought of them at all until now; too swept up in the whirlwind that was turning out to be her life currently. "Why not just make another key?" She asked as she settled onto the couch.

"We can't." Khandra said, "The art of the keys is long lost. As is most of history regarding them. Wiped out by the Holy Land in their pursuit of being the one to control the narrative." She pursed her lips while shaking her head slightly. "Donovan left here with the key that would take him from our realm to yours, as well as the key that would bring him back."

"There are two keys for both realms. Like a door with a different lock on each side." Davion held his hand up at the door and poked each side to drive home the point. "He wanted to keep the realms separated. Leaving the Earth key in your realm cuts us off from the Earth realm... Clearly."

"What if the fae who went to my world had found a way there to make more keys?" Belle asked, sitting a little straighter while clinging to the thin thread of hope.

Khandra shrugged. "Perhaps they had. How else would we receive stories of your realm the same way that your realm has received stories of ours? It is near certain that The Holy Land has erased as much of the lore that surrounds it; therefore, the magic is lost." She waved the thought away. "Unfortunately, we have to operate under the thought that the key from our realm to yours is now lost in your realm, as it was not on Donovan when he was recovered."

Belle's blood ran cold; she felt like all the air had been knocked from her lungs. The only hope of ever getting home was just as lost to Belle as Donovan was now. He probably had the key stashed in his safe room in his fancy penthouse in New York. Belle had probably seen it a thousand times over and never thought anything of it... Not that it mattered now. Neither Donovan nor Belle would ever see that penthouse again. Her posture faltered as she stared out into the distance, giving herself a moment to think about everything that had changed.

Davion shifted his gaze down to Belle at his side, noticing the way that her shoulders dropped, and her body seemed to deflate. Davion rolled his wrist and three glasses, and a decorative bottle appeared wrapped in his delicate dark smoke and carried to them, already filled, and the decanter was placed on the table between them. Belle made a small noise before pressing the glass to her lips and once again downing it in one go.

They stayed and chatted well into the night, the sun had long set, and the moon was high in the sky when Khandra had finally run out of questions about Belle's realm; and so long as Davion continued to supply her with alcohol, Belle was content in answering, her mind once again distracted and unable to process everything in her world. Part of her didn't even want to process now; she just wanted to survive.

"I feel like I am in a fairytale..." Belle confessed on the walk back to her quarters. Catching the look he sent her, she couldn't help but laugh slightly, shaking her head as she leaned into his side. "I wonder if that's where the name comes from... Someone from this world in my world... Fantastical stories of princes and princesses, fae folk, magic, all things that weren't real in my world."

"What would be works of fiction in your world," Davion said, his voice low beside her ear, "...could have been truths from mine."

Belle's brows furrowed, but she nodded faintly. He adjusted his arm around her waist to keep them steady as they walked. "Too much fae wine, little one..." Belle giggled and nodded once more, leaning into him.

"Mother will want you gone when we tell her that you have no power and that it must have been because of Donovan that you came through the portal." He drank just as much as Belle and Khandra had, and the only one in a state was Belle. "She cannot know the truth. She will send you away immediately, if not kill you outright. She will think you have sway over me." His jaw tightened because part of him wondered if maybe she did. "It's what happened to the other kingdoms." Belle rolled her eyes and slumped her shoulders slightly.

"Our only option is to tell her that you are my pretty little plaything..." There was a dark, playful tone in his voice, but when Belle shot him a glare, he couldn't help but grin. "Your anger aside, you would look breathtaking covered in my marks..." They had stopped walking without Belle noticing. Davion stepped in, backing her against the wall, stalking toward her as if she were a rabbit cornered by a predator. His body pressed to hers, inching her dress higher with deliberate slowness.

"You have enough fire to keep up with me, little one..." He cooed, his mouth just inches from hers. "Every step you took would remind you, and anyone watching, exactly who you belonged to. My marks on your skin, my scent clinging to you..."

Belle's breath caught in her throat, and it took every bit of willpower and restraint for her not to spread her legs for him. Instead, she leaned forward, catching his bottom lip between hers and sucked in lightly before biting down, the iron taste of blood coating her tongue as he jerked away with a curse, instinctively raising a hand to slap her. He stopped and laughed, wiping his bottom lip. "Little minx... the harder you fight me... The harder I am going to fuck you when I finally can." He stepped up and trailed a finger down her jawline to

47

the tip, forcing her to look up at him. "I am going to ruin you..."

Belle let out a light laugh and pushed off the wall, grabbing handfuls of her skirts and shaking them to straighten them out before continuing their walk to her quarters. "You can try..." She shrugged lightly before looking over her shoulder. "I know the rest of the way." Flicking her hair over her shoulder, "You can go brood, or do whatever princely things you do." She waved a dismissive hand at him while shaking her head and laughing.

Davion stayed rooted, watching the wonderfully infuriating woman disappear down the corridor, his lip still throbbing. Surely the pull of her magic hadn't worn off yet. That had to be why he wanted to chase her, pin her, and fuck her until she was screaming his name. It was because she was a succubus. It had to be. Not the sharpness in her gaze when she challenged him. Not the way that she tasted like danger and defiance. And certainly not because, somewhere deep in the parts of himself he'd rather burn away, he already knew that she was going to matter, and maybe she did already.

He growled low in his throat, clenched his jaw, and turned on his heel.

Chapter 7

There were platters of food in her quarters when she returned. She was certain the Queen had made sure to try to keep her under lock and key, minus the lock, and even likely had said something along the lines about hiding the trash. Belle relaxed, chatting with Maude and Sadie, well, the best that she could with Maude's ever watchful eye, knowing that Sadie was the one who would give her any information about any of the off-the-wall questions she could come up with. Maude seemed very old school, very proper, and in some ways, Belle assumed that she was. Sadie was younger, both physically and in the way she had quietly become a friend of Belle's rather than just a handmaid.

The moon rose high into the sky, a beaming soft, white light through the tall, arched windows. By now, both Sadie and Maude had long retired to what Belle quietly assumed was a bunked room with many of the other staff of the castle. Who could blame her? She didn't have anything except her world's fiction to go by. She stared into the fire for a while as she sipped on some fae wine, the strong stuff that Davion had given her upon arrival in this weird realm.

It felt like any time Belle had a breath, even a heartbeat to herself, something inside of her wanted to cry out. Part of her wanted to scream at the top of her lungs and mourn the fact that her best friend had been left in a field to die. Another part of Belle was curious about what her life was becoming; was she meant to be a plaything to Davion? What was her plan? Did she still want to look for a way to escape when all she had been told was that there was no way back to her world? And even if

49

she could make it back to her world... what would be left there for her?

Once the alcohol had brought a flush back to her cheeks and caused her head to swim, Belle headed to bed, wiping away an errant tear that she hadn't even realized had fallen. Tucking herself in, Belle lay on her side facing the door, carefully tucking the blade Davion had given her under her pillow. Part of her half-expected Davion to have to come see her. It was the first time he had left her alone for more than a couple of hours, and a silent truth that she would never admit out loud was that it made her feel a little hollow.

Sighing deeply, Belle drifted off to sleep with her fingers curled around the handle of the small blade, staying at the ready now that she knew she was public enemy number one.

When dreams finally came to her, she saw Donovan lying in a field, bleeding out as he watched the portal close with Belle screaming out for him. The dream twisted and showed Belle Donovan's decaying body, left in the field for no one to ever find, for no one to lay his body to rest. She dreamed of Davion having secret meetings with his mother where they whispered horrible things about Belle, and how they would use her and her abilities to topple other kingdoms the same way that the succubi used to do for themselves in the past.

Belle swatted at her face, feeling a tickling that started at her brows and ran down the tip of her nose. The same sensation happened a second time, slowly pulling Belle back to the waking world, saving her from her own dreams. When she finally opened her eyes, Khandra was lying in Belle's bed on her stomach, arms propped up on her elbows, smiling mischievously in the dimly lit room. "Get up, silly... It's party time." She all but sang before running her index finger down Belle's nose once more. "As you are currently, tragically, styled by my brother, therefore, I come bearing gifts." She rolled off the bed and glided over to a pile of varying fabrics on the couch.

Belle rubbed her eyes as she slowly sat up, her gaze following Khandra as she practically bounced around the room. "I also have party favors." Khandra gave a little wiggle before pulling a small vial out of her cleavage. "Think of it like the fae wine... But, much... much better." Belle lofted a brow and couldn't help but smile at how excited Khandra seemed to be; it was infectious. "Come on, come on, come on. It will royally piss Davion off, aren't you all for that?" A laugh passed Belle's lips now as she nodded and extended her hand to Khandra. "Yes!" Khandra bounced back over to Belle, pulling her out of bed, playfully and grandly spinning Belle under her arm as if they were dancing before handing her the vial of swirling silver liquid. It glittered in the dim light of Belle's room, swirling of its own volition, looking almost like a bedazzled storm cloud. "Let's get you ready first. Don't want you to lose it before you even make it to where we are going."

With her hands free, Khandra wiggled back over to the clothes that were bunched up on the couch and began digging through the pile. She dropped some on the floor while muttering to herself, throwing others on the chair across from the couch as her 'maybe' pile.

The excited whirlwind that was Khandra in full party mode had Belle dressed in a tiny black number within minutes. It tied at the back of her neck and crossed at her collarbones, plunging low at her breasts. Forming an X at her ribs as the fabric curled back at her spine, where it became the shortest skirt with tiny pleats to give it a flare. Khandra sat Belle down at the vanity and began toying with her hair, rambling that Belle would want it out of her face because it was going to get hot.

"Tell me about Donovan." Belle interrupted, bringing Khandra to a complete standstill as she looked at Belle through the mirror. There was heartache in Belle's voice, and Khandra couldn't help but feel awful for her.

"Another time." She decided with a nod before clearing her throat. "Tonight is about forgetting all of these problems." With a little triumphant squeal, Khandra gave Belle's shoulders a little squeeze before nodding toward the standing mirror.

As Belle approached the mirror, Khandra wiggled another little silver vial loose from her cleavage and waited for Belle to inspect herself. It had been years since Belle had been to any nightclub or bar, or anything that would call for such a brazen outfit, but she was here for it. "Bottoms up. Enjoy the Silver, love." Khandra called while popping the little cork out of the vial and tipping her head back, waving a hand for Belle to do the same.

With a little shrug, Belle flicked the cork from the vial and followed behind Khandra. It was surprisingly sweet and went down with a gentle cooling sensation. "It will kick in by the time we get there. Come on!" Khandra linked arms with Belle and practically pulled her until Belle had her feet under her. With her steps stabled, she was able to keep up with Khandra as they ran through the halls, skipping and giggling all the way down to the grounds and out a small gate that Belle was certain was reserved for those who worked in the castle.

This was the first time she had been outside of the castle, and if she had been in her right mind, she would have been paying better attention to the direction they'd taken. She glanced over her shoulder, catching her first real look at the grand structure in all its glory. Towers clawed at the sky, their tips wreathed in moonlight, and a wall thick as a fortress wrapped around the grounds. Beautiful, yes, but beauty didn't make the stones any less of a cage. Those walls weren't just there to keep enemies out. They were there to keep people like Belle in.

They skipped and slid down a grassy hill into what looked like the forest Belle had seen beyond the gardens. The further they weaved through the trees, the lighter Belle felt; all worries, fears and cares slipped away with each step they took. Soon enough, both women could hear a deep pulsing beat further into the forest, "Nearly there." Khandra said, laughing,

Bursting into the clearing in the trees felt more like they had just walked into a bubble. Suddenly, the music was booming, loud drums, flutes, and violins playing some sort of joyful music that filled all of Belle's senses. Khandra held onto Belle's hand as they weaved through the crowd of dancing fae, placing themselves in the middle of it all. Belle was too awestruck, her senses overloaded as the Silver fully took hold of her. She could feel the music deep within her body. The sweeping movement of the bow of the violin, slowly bringing her hips to sway in time, or the lilting pull and song of the flutes, and the deep thumping beat of the drums that became the heartbeat of the crowd.

A beautiful fae woman wearing hardly any clothing walked by with a tray of glasses filled with the swirling silver liquid, and Khandra snagged two before getting Belle's attention. With an airy laugh, Belle accepted it and toasted Khandra before drinking the entire glass with her. The magical cooling sensation was dulled as Belle felt a warm body come up behind her, gentle fingers whispering at her exposed side before sliding down to her lower abdomen, pressing her back, a few feet away from Khandra, who was already distracted by a handsy dancer, who was clearly also under the influence of the magic silver liquid.

Soon enough, wandering hands trailed across Belle's spine, whispering the gentlest touch at Belle's exposed ribs, spreading themselves around to her stomach before pulling her back and away from Khandra. Belle's hips continued to sway as her hands went above her head before reaching back to touch the neck of the person who was guiding their sway. Their bodies pressed together as the music around them seemed to build and breathe, moving with the packed crowd around the blazing fire. There was no room for words amongst them, just bodies and beats as the entire crowd moved with the music; everyone's pupils as dilated as Khandra's and Belle's, likely from whatever the delicious magic liquid was.

The hands that held Belle against the muscular frame behind her wandered slightly, one hand dangerously low on her abdomen, guiding their movements with his fingertips to move them to the right, and the base of his palm to ease them to the left. His left hand trailed north, between her breasts, gently over the black fabric, before his hand found her throat, where his thumb stroked gently at the edge of Belle's jaw. She leaned her body against him, exhaling while fluttering her eyes closed as he leaned down to her neck, slowly inhaling her scent before placing kisses just under her ear, spreading them gently in time with the music and moving them to her shoulder, bringing Belle to curl her fingers into his shaggy hair.

She continued to move with the mystery man, his touch sparking a strange sense of familiarity, one that not only should be impossible. One that was impossible. A thread of panic curled in her chest, but was smoothed away, forcing her breathing to match the rhythm of the music. Whatever ghosts her mind wanted to summon, she shoved them back in the dark. She would never feel that again. Not here. Not now.

She opened her eyes just in time to see the hand of the man Khandra was dancing with slide up under her skirt, earning him a moan as Khandra arched her back and leaned against him. Belle took the hand at her throat and guided it along her sternum before allowing him to cup her breast, her hand squeezed over his, letting her head fall against his chest, exhaling a delightful sigh... A sigh that started a tiny wave across the crowd.

The beat of the music shifted to something with a low bass that rumbled through Belle's chest; the pyre in the center of it all sparked a vibrant green color. Belle gasped and stared at the fire, mesmerized for a moment before the hand at her breast shifted back to her throat, tilting her head back, while using their thumb to coax her mouth open. She moved fluidly under his touch and smiled with her eyes as he poured another vial of the silver liquid into her mouth. He draped a piece of fabric over Belle's eyes, tying it to the back of her head gently before feathering her neck with a few more kisses, trailing across her throat to the other side as well. Taking her hand in his, he took a step back and twirled her under his arm a few times.

The movement was so freeing that she laughed even while using her free hand to hold the fabric in place, spinning just fast enough that the lovely updo in her long brown hair came free, flowing just as freely as she felt. The man pulled Belle back to him and lifted her easily, holding his hands at her ass cheeks when she wrapped her legs around him as they continued to spin and move to the beat of the music. Belle only took the blindfold off to rest her hands on his shoulders, watching as the treetops spun with her, the stars twirled and danced as they continued to move, and for the first time since falling into this world, Belle felt a sense of happiness.

Khandra watched as Belle laughed, genuinely laughed; it brought a smile to her lips. Khandra was always a keeper of secrets; it was part of what made her so quietly powerful amongst the court, and why no one ever bothered her. She caught the eye of the man spinning Belle, and gave him a silent, knowing nod, before tilting her chin up toward the castle. He returned the nod and soon set Belle's feet back to the ground, spinning her away from him, toward Khandra before vanishing into the night.

Time flew by; the beats of the music, mixed with the ever-changing fire and free-flowing silver liquid, had Belle floating. She danced with anyone who came her way, allowing hands to freely wander. She had forgotten entirely about Khandra, about the insanity of the past few days; Donovan, Davion, all of it had faded away in the bliss of the night.

Khandra bound up to Belle as she finished off another vial. "Fuck Davion!" She pumped her arm in the air, and Belle laughed, following the motion of throwing her fist high into the air as Khandra fell onto her, resulting in riotous laughter from both.

"Fuck that stuck up grump!" Belle cheered and hoisted herself up onto a table, pulling Khandra with her. Cheers erupted as the two women danced, bodies pressed against one another to the point of being purely sexual. A third woman joined them, sandwiching Belle in the middle, pouring the silver liquid in Belle's mouth. What drops of the Silver magic that Belle missed were licked off Belle's stomach by Khandra. So high on whatever was in the spelled drink, Belle let out another quiet moan, too engrossed in the fun to notice the shockwave of pleasure that rippled from her to the crowd closest to the table. Sweaty bodies glistening in the dim light grew closer to one another, the beat of the music dropped to something with a little more swing to it, whoever was already grinding on another seemed to pull each other a little tighter as the invisible wave washed through the entire warded bubble. Pleasured exhales escaped parted lips, hard bodies grew more tense, and what started as a simple handsy dance began to evolve into something a little darker; as if on cue, the fire dimmed to a deep, dark red.

Outside of the warded area of the forest, far across the grounds that Khandra and Belle had run through, deep in the bowels of the castle, Cortland had appeared to Davion, informing him of a disturbance in the forest. Begrudgingly, he rose from his bed, dressed, and grabbed two blades, ready for whatever bullshit Courtland had decided was important enough to bring to his attention in the dead of night.

Courtland guided Davion to the edge of the woods, the faintest flickering light deep in the tree line, and a sensual rhythmic bass emanated from the trees. "Straight ahead, sire."

55

Then he vanished without saying anything else or even asking permission to leave. Davion took a deep breath and stepped into the thick of the forest.

The woman behind Belle had taken to kissing her neck. Their bodies still moving in time with the beat of the music, as if the entire party were under some sexual spell, heaving, writhing, moaning, and grunting, starting quietly around them. Belle's head fell back, her damp hair sticking to her mostly exposed back as she granted the woman better access and breathed a pleased sigh.

A thick, sharp, dark vine snapped its way around Belle's waist, shocking her back to reality before yanking her roughly off the table. She let out a pained grunt before stumbling forward, trying to keep her feet under her so the vine did not drag her across the dirt. "Just what in the hell do you think you are doing?" Davion snapped in her face, catching her by the throat as the vine pulled Belle directly to him.

"Mmm..." She trailed a hand up from his stomach to his chest, her lips curling into a pleased smile, "The party police have arrived..." she pouted, her eyes glossy and dilated to the point they looked black in place of their typical light brown. Ignoring the tightening hand at her throat, she tried to look back at Khandra, trying to send the princess a warning that he had come to ruin their night. Davion huffed out an annoyed breath before jerking her attention back to him.

"What did she give you, Belle?" His eyes burned into her, but when she smiled and simply tilted her head back to loosen his grip, Davion slapped her, not hard enough to hurt, but enough to catch her attention.

"Silver..." Her voice sounded more like a song than an answer. Belle's wandering hands pulled his shirt loose from his pants, inching it higher, egging him to take it off. "Don't you want to dance with me, Davion?" She spread her palms along his bare stomach now, slowly sliding them higher on his torso, all but sending shivers up her own body as she felt every muscle tense when she touched him. Belle locked her eyes on Davion's now, her turn to take his jaw in her hand and force him to look at her instead of scanning the crowd for Khandra. "Don't you want to fuck me, Davion?" The words practically poured from her as she searched his eyes. He didn't need to answer, nor did he need to hide his feelings with a mask of anger as he narrowed his eyes at Belle. She could feel his desire; it burned brighter than the fire at her back. The hand that did not hold him steady slid back down his body, loosening the ties of his pants before easing its way in. She half expected him to stop her; instead, he stood still, taking a steadying breath as Belle's fingers wrapped around his hard length.

As if unable to give up power, Davion readjusted the hand at her throat, and Belle brought her hand to his wrist. He leaned in, for a second, Belle thought he would kiss her, but instead, he spoke through gritted teeth. "You forget what you are... You don't even know what you are capable of..." With a quick jerk of his arm, he spun her to face the crowd before yanking her back hard against his body, preventing her from escaping his grip. He snaked his other hand around her midsection, the tips of his fingers just inside the upper hem of the skirt at her hip. "Do you see all of these people?" He questioned while tightening his grip on her throat, slowly bending his wrist to make her scan the entire crowd.

What had started as a wild dance party in the woods, consisting of all kinds of fae folk from all backgrounds, had progressed into an all-out orgy. There were bodies and limbs everywhere, groupings of people tangled together, hands pawing and clawing at anyone within their grasp. Bodies thrusting in time with the music, moans muffled by mixed kisses or busied mouths. "This is you, Belle... This is what you're doing..." He pressed his hard length into her ass cheeks, "As is this." Her eyes fluttered shut, and she rocked her hips back into him intentionally, biting her lower lip before wiggling slightly.

"Come on, Davion, no one would notice if we joined in..." She tugged at his wrist roughly, breaking its grip on her throat enough for her to spin to face him. Before she could hear any more protests or bullshit about her being a danger and her bringing forth an orgy in a ward-protected party in the forest. She stepped up onto her toes while wrapping her hands around the back of his head, pushing him forward. For a split second when their lips met, Davion didn't move, didn't react, but as

Belle leaned her entire body into him, trailing her tongue at his lower lip before nipping it, his resolve cracked then.

Davion shook his head slightly before their lips crashed together once more. As another small moan escaped from Belle's lips, she opened just enough for him to slide his tongue into her mouth; she sucked at his tongue lightly, swirling her tongue around his as she pressed her nails into his shoulders. He gripped her hips so tightly that Belle was sure there would be bruises; she shivered, and she let her head fall back momentarily as she moaned his name in a whisper. Another wave crashed over the crowd, and they all echoed her moan with one of their own. Giving her a moment to breathe, Davion blinked a few times, his vision blurring slightly; the only thing he was able to see clearly was Belle. "Ruin me..." She begged while grinding against him, "Do your worst..." She encouraged him, and it earned a low growl as he leaned in and bit down on her shoulder. The sound that escaped from Belle dripped with pleasure and pain; the wave of power tore through everyone else a bit more sharply now, a few falling over their own edges.

It was contained to this crowd only, he thought to himself in a moment of clarity before looking up between the trees. Davion could see the faintest shimmer of the barrier's magic; it was contained, he reminded himself. There hadn't been succubi or incubi in the kingdom since he was a young boy, but the effects, especially if not contained, could be devastating, and now Davion was poised to ruin one here and now. "Fine..." His eyes darkened as his attention shifted back to Belle. "Since you're begging like a little whore..." He brought his hand back to her throat and forced her back against the nearest tree, the rough bark biting into her back as their lips crashed together once more. "Remember when you're begging me to stop... You wanted this..."

Belle looked up at him with a coy smile, nodding before licking her lips, "Yes, your highness..." She purred between kisses before his lips trailed to her throat and neck. He could taste the same sweetness of the Silver there as he cupped her breasts into his hands. He bit and sucked at the crook of her neck, bruising her fresh.

"Take it off." He muttered before biting once more. Belle released the tie at the back of her neck, and the front crossed straps of the dress fell, the strings dangling by her feet. "All of it, Belle." There was a dangerous tone in his voice as he stepped back to look at her. Belle shimmied the skirt to the ground and stood with her back against the tree. She watched as he took her in; he needed to look at her in all her beauty under the moonlight. With a sharp inhale, he pulled his shirt over his head, letting it hit the ground somewhere near her dress before diving back into her breasts, his hand working up between her thighs. He found her core, wet and ready, and when he trailed his fingers around her clit the crowd erupted in moans, but his entire focus was on Belle as she cried out, moaning while pressing her back against the tree while wrapping a leg around him. He slid his fingers deep into her pussy, stroking that sweet spot until her knees shook. Davion stood straight, forcing Belle to look at him. She licked his thumb, and he appeased her desire by sliding his thumb into her mouth, watching her intently as she sucked on it as if it were his cock instead of a finger. "Good girl... Come for me... All over my fingers... Good girl..." The praise was the trigger, she moaned out against him, panting through parted lips, writhing and rocking her hips against his hand.

He gave her absolutely no room to recover from her orgasm and grabbed her lifted leg with one hand while grabbing his length in the other, drilling into her. She cried out and her whole body jerked as she dug her nails into his shoulders. He was huge, and she was so very full. His stroke was perfect, pulling himself out to the tip before thrusting hard enough to make her breath hitch. It was that sweet pain that she craved as he bottomed out in her. Davion fucked her hard and fast, drilling deep into her with each thrust, lost entirely in the way that her body reacted to him.

She felt like bliss wrapped around him. Davion grunted with each thrust, determined to both please and hurt Belle; he wanted to leave his mark on her, and he wanted to give her more. She was the only thing on his mind, the only thing he could see, the only thing he could feel. The intense need he felt for Belle was all consuming, blinding. The more she moaned, the harder he fucked her, their bodies slapping together as Belle quickly climbed to her next orgasm. Without warning, he pulled out, stepping back from Belle, watching as she collapsed onto her knees at the base of the tree.

Grabbing her by the hair, he knelt with her, turning her around and pushing her face into the dirt. A loud crack gave a slight echo as he smacked her ass, a red handprint forming almost instantly. He dove back into her, mentally obsessing with her smooth skin, the pale color it took on in the moonlight as her back arched, pressing her chest further into the dirt. With her hair still wrapped in his hand, he jerked her up, holding her off the ground by her hair alone. "Cry for me..." He urged, while he thrust hard and deep into her, he wanted her pain, he wanted her pleasure, Davion wanted everything.

Her dirt-stained cheeks were flushed now more than they had been from the Silver, bright red as she gasped and panted and moaned for him, for Davion. He silenced her by bringing his free hand from her hip to her mouth, clamping down hard over her plump lips, forcing what little air she could through her nose alone. The lack of free breathing had her head swimming, her eyes rolling back in her head.

When he released her, she fell forward into the dirt, just barely catching herself on her hands as his hands gripped her hips tighter than a vice, adding more bruises on top of the others that would surely form because of him, and Belle welcomed each and every mark.

Somewhere in the distance, the crowd was losing their minds to an unseen force of sexual ecstasy, and perhaps Davion and Belle were too, but they would welcome being swallowed by the madness.

He pushed down on her back, forcing her to arch just a bit further, her face resting on her fingers, before he grabbed at her hands, pulling her wrists high up on her back, twisting her arms so she could do nothing but take it, her face in the dirt once again. She did what she could to grab his wrists, holding on for dear life as he mercilessly fucked her. With a small shift of her arms, he pulled her face out of the dirt again, using her wrists to anchor him, to continue at the brutal pace. Her head went limp as she fell through another orgasm, muscles burning as she cried out his name between ragged breaths. His name cried out from her lips in the throes of such violent passion, was the final straw; he couldn't hold on any longer. He pushed her down into the dirt, caging her small body under his as he poured into her, slowing his pace before finally stopping, gasping on top of her.

Reality slowly crept back in for them both; the burning red light of the fire faded, the crowd quieted, left to heaving breaths and gasps for air, bodies tangled around the fire. Davion rolled off Belle, but before his back could hit the dirt, both of them were engulfed by the black smoke and dropped onto the bed of her quarters. Belle let out a small sound of approval upon feeling the softness of the bed and blankets under her, far too spent to be concerned with the dirt that clung to her sweaty body. "It's like you're dangerous to me ..." he muttered while closing his eyes.

Chapter 8

Belle barely moved after Davion fell asleep next to her, one arm tucked under his head, naked under the thin dark sheet that covered him from the waist down. Part of her didn't want to move; she knew so many parts of her body would be sore once the Silver finally wore off. So perfectly, blissfully sore. However, pleasure was a dangerous indulgence here. Every moment she allowed herself to forget where she was, and who she shared a bed with, was another step toward giving him an advantage she couldn't afford.

Yet all she could do was stare at him; as much as she could see Donovan, she could separate the two, aside from the obvious. There was a certain brooding air to Davion that Donovan didn't possess; it held tight to the way he carried himself, and it didn't just stem from the regal upbringing. Their physical attributes were very similar; of course, they were twins. However, their toned, muscular build would lead anyone to believe that they had trained together, which, in another life, they may have, in another life that wouldn't have separated them.

"I can feel you staring at me, Belle." He muttered before licking his lower lip. She wrinkled her nose and shifted her eyes past him, across the long room to the fireplace. "I can see why your kind were taken away..." Belle couldn't help but roll her eyes and prop her head up on her hand.

"So not only do your people" she emphasized with as much sass as she could, "make verbal stabs at those that you see as lesser, you're also going to refer to my kind as something that is hush hush and shunned?" Belle scoffed and pushed herself off the bed, snatching the thin, silken robe off one of the posts of the bed, swinging it onto her arms in one fluid motion.

"Do you ever not bite at people?" He asked while pushing himself up to his elbows, watching her like a wolf as she stormed around the room, removing the pointless pins from her hair, releasing her glorious brown curls fully.

"If you feel my truths are bites, you're in for a rude awakening if you ever actually piss me off." Davion quirked a brow at her words and just how easily they fell from her mouth, without a care that she was speaking to royalty. "I think you are too familiar with living in this castle, having everyone cower at your presence; and now that you're stuck with me, and I don't give a flying fuck about your title, or your crown, that it shakes you to actually have someone throw truth at you..." She sat on the edge of the bed, and Davion rolled toward her, eyes still glued to her. "I'm sure I've had more interaction with the people you're meant to rule than you have had in a long time, and they were all dancing with me, pressing their bodies against me..." She was tactical with what she knew could get a rise out of him. His jaw tensed, Belle fought back the urge to grin, "Hands all over me..." She mocked, running her hands up her thighs, watching as his storm grey eyes followed her hands as they moved up her stomach, over her breasts, to her throat.

That's when he pounced. Davion sprang up from his position and pinned Belle to the bed, swatting her hand away from her throat and replacing it with his own as he straddled her waist. "What happened the last time you teased me, Belle..." He growled while lowering his face to hers, crowding her view, refusing to have her look at anything but him. Even as he tightened his grip on her throat, her lips parted, and the corners turned into a sly smile.

"I can't tell if you're obsessed with me... Or if I'm coming into the power of my kind," she quipped through limited breath. He huffed out a grunt and pushed from her, stepping back from the bed. It was Belle who watched him like prey now, watching how his hands flexed and tightened into white knuckled fists and back, how his jaw ticked, how he rolled his shoulders as if shaking off some tension. She pressed up to her elbows, "Going to run to mommy and tell her my dirty little secret?" Belle pouted. "Tell her the dirty little succubus tricked you and was being mean to you?" She could see Davion struggling with himself; there was a war in his own mind, of what his reaction to her provocation should be, and Belle reveled in it.

Davion didn't even move, but the black vines snapped around her ankles as they dangled from the bed and yanked her down, her knees slamming hard down on the floor. His eyes flashed dark as he stormed back up to Belle, grabbing his cock, stroking it slowly, "You talk too much..." He growled before swiping the back of his hand across her face with a loud crack. Her cheek reddened almost instantly, but it got the result he wanted; her mouth opened, and Davion seized that small moment to shove his cock in. There was no protest from Belle, her lips clasped around him as he rocked his hips, thrusting into her mouth. "I think I like you on your knees, Belle." He grunted his words while tangling his hand in her hair, forcing her to take more of him even as he continued to thrust into her mouth.

For her own stability, Belle wrapped her hands around his thighs, using them as an anchor as she willingly gave him her mouth and her throat, keeping her eyes locked to him. "No." He shook his head slightly, and another set of vines snatched her wrists and pulled them up behind her, holding them in place against the mattress, twisting her shoulders sharply. The burn in her shoulders was almost instant. Belle sat up a little taller on her knees, gargling a moan as she pulled against the vines, craving her freedom from the growing pain in her shoulders.

Davion watched as Belle grimaced and arched her back, knowing full well the pain her current position was causing. "Can you taste your pussy on my cock?" His free hand stroked her cheek gently. Not that he gave her any room to respond, let alone take a full breath, Belle gave a slight nod and used the tip of her tongue to glide along his length as he continued to fuck her mouth. Drool eased out of the corners of her lips, and tears welled in her eyes, but if anything, Belle wasn't a quitter.

He pulled his cock out of her mouth, leaning back just far enough for the bead of saliva to stretch from her mouth to the tip of his dick, and with a sadistic grin, he slapped her again, this time on the opposite cheek. "Look how quiet you've become, filthy little whore..." Her nails dug into the sheets, balled into tight fists; she opened her mouth to cuss back, but once again, he took advantage of her open mouth, shoving himself back in, thrusting roughly forward before lingering there, preventing her ability to breathe. When a tear slipped freely down her face, he backed away, allowing her a moment to breathe. Her chest heaved high as she sucked in a clear breath, only to have it cut off by him diving in once more. "Finally found a good use for your mouth." He ground out his words, one hand holding the wood of the four-post bed, the other on the back of her head, forcing her to take all of him. She moaned against him, the slight vibration toppling his last bit of control, sending a shiver straight down his spine. "Good... fucking... girl..." He spilled down her throat, stilling for a moment as his vision blurred.

Belle wasted no time; Davion stopped moving, and Belle started. Slow, agonizing movements, trailing her tongue around his length before twirling it teasingly around his head, causing Davion to buck against her involuntarily. When she continued to move, he yanked her back hard by her hair, pulling her off him, too sensitive to take much more. "Go to bed. We start training in the morning. I expect no complaints about the lack of sleep. You were the one who decided to go out with my sister." The vines released, and her arms fell limply, fingers tingling as circulation slowly came back. "Sadie will have pants for you." A whoosh of black smoke, and Davion was gone. She narrowed her eyes at the space that he had just taken up, shaking her head slightly before rolling her shoulders, wincing.

In the quiet of his quarters, Davion sat by the fire, a drink clasped between his hands as he leaned forward, elbows on his knees as he stared into the flames as if they held the answers he was searching for. The fire in the hearth burned low, casting soft orange flickers around the room, but his pulse still pounded like a war drum. His body hummed, blood thrumming with an energy that wasn't just his own.

Belle's magic still clung to him. It hadn't faded, not even after he left her room, not even after he crossed most of the castle to his quarters. He could still taste her, feel her lips on his skin, feel the pull like a hook behind his ribs. The moment their mouths met at the rave, something snapped into place. It wasn't just an attraction. It wasn't just lust; it was something much deeper than that, and it consumed Davion's thoughts. He felt like she was the only thing in the world, that she was the only thing he could see clearly, and everything else blurred around him.

Davion had seen the tangles of his people when he came into the clearing in the woods, assuming at first it was only the effects of the Silver and a wild night. But when he saw his sister trail her tongue up Belle's stomach to catch the Silver, and he watched as Belle's head fell back in a moment of euphoria, not only did he see that pleasure expand across the crowd, but he also felt it ripple through him. The people bent and folded around to the waves Belle was releasing, how the fae lost themselves in lust, pulled into the storm Belle had unknowingly summoned. That was no ordinary desire. That was power; ancient, hungry, and dangerous, and it belonged to Belle.

Some dark part of Davion wanted to claim that power for himself. Not to control and wield it recklessly as so many before him had attempted to do, but to drown in it. Like an addict constantly craving more.

This... this is why the incubi and succubi were hunted. Not because they were evil, but because one touch could bend the will of kings and crumble empires. And for a moment... he had wanted to be bent. Davion hated to admit it, but he still wanted to bend.

He let out a breath, slow and shaky, running his thumb along the edge of his jaw. His hands weren't trembling anymore, but something inside him was. He finished off the glass of fae wine, willing it to calm the nerves that no one could touch.

He couldn't lose himself. Not like this. Davion had to find the edge of that blade and learn how to walk it. Because if he gave in to Belle completely, if he let her power make his decisions for him, he'd be no better than the weak, twisted rulers who let desire destroy their judgment. The same rulers who had once carried the weight of the realm on their shoulders had been toppled and torn to shreds by the sexual power of another. It could not be Davion. It would not be.

And yet... Gods, he still wanted her. Even now, he was fighting the urge to return to her room, to taste her again, to drown in the heat that made him forget who he was. If he was going to keep his crown, if he was going to be the ruler this realm needed... He had to learn how to want her and not be undone by her.

Chapter 9

Sadie gently nudged Belle's arm and was lazily swatted away in return. "M'la–" She began before quickly correcting herself, "Belle," Belle's eyes popped open. She knew they were alone if Sadie wasn't standing on parade. "You've got to get up, breakfast is in your sitting area, as is your outfit for the day. His Highness requests your presence in one of the training towers. I will assist you in getting ready and escort you." Belle scrubbed her hands over her face before sitting up, wincing slightly at the various pains and strains across her body, especially in her damned shoulders.

"You are all going to make me fat... I haven't eaten this much, probably ever..." She muttered while grabbing the sheet and wrapping it around herself, pulling it clear off the bed with her. Shuffling over to the silver tray, lined with muffins, fruit, and bowls of yogurt. Part of Belle felt that Davion choosing this morning of all mornings to 'train' was a secondary part of her punishment; he knew how her body would feel with her arms having been cranked back at such an awkward angle the night before, and he still chose this morning for them to train. "Sadie..." Belle practically whined while patting the couch next to her when she plopped down on the couch. "Sit with me, please." Sadie glanced around the room before nodding, lowering herself, almost cautiously, onto the couch next to Belle, anxiously adjusting her skirts. "What the hell am I doing here?" Belle motioned grandly at the room, but the quizzical look it gained her from Sadie made her elaborate. "Why am I here? I was essentially taken prisoner, but Davion doesn't exactly treat me like a prisoner... the Queen..." She huffed out

68

a breath and rolled her eyes, "Well, we can tell where she stands with me being here, and if that's the case, why hasn't she kicked me out yet?"

Belle sipped at a warm glass of tea before taking a bite of a strawberry, watching as Sadie tried to calculate her answer. "No one knows." It came out quick and short, like a secret she hadn't meant to tell. "The entire staff is just as confused as you are." She pulled her lips tight and looked at the door. "Your entire situation is a mystery to us. No one has mentioned a motive. A few of us think that the royal Prince has become smitten with you. He has given you more attention in the short time you have been here than he has given anyone in a very, very long time. Some think you have ties to the Traitor..." Belle narrowed her eyes, and Sadie zipped up again. Shaking her head, Belle went back to eating. "The Queen has already asked for your removal, or to have you marked as property of Davion, so that she can justify you being here. You would be properly moved into his quarters and be at his beck and call." Belle huffed as she bit into a muffin. "As that has not happened, there are no solid answers."

She nodded slowly before wiping her hands on the sheet that covered her. "That just gives me more questions than answers..." She let her body collapse back against the couch they sat on with a large sigh. "If you were a prisoner, why be granted hospitality? Why allow you to be trained in whatever magic you have? Why make a prisoner more powerful?" Belle pointed to Sadie before tapping her temple and nodding, more to herself than to Sadie. "They want to use my abilities..." Belle stilled, her chest hurting slightly at the thought that Davion only wanted to keep her here to keep his kingdom's power or use her to topple another. "Not they... Just him..." It had to be why Davion was also so adamant about his mother not knowing about Belle's abilities. Nodding a little, Belle decided that she needed to fight Davion now.

Standing and letting the sheet fall to the floor, Belle pulled the pants on. They were dull, black leather and, of course, they fit like a glove, everything having been made specifically for Belle. She shook her head at the loose-fitting top; it was the same dark blue that marked her as Davion's. It had a small thin string that weaved back and forth down the center of her chest.

When she turned to Sadie, she was already holding a corset, this one different from the others. She shrugged this one on like it was a vest before standing with her hands on her hips, allowing Sadie to strap her in. "Not too tight, please... I'm ready for a fight, and the more I can move, the better it will be." Belle pleaded, and Sadie obliged, pulling the straps tight enough to feather the hem of the shirt and draw Belle's breasts together.

"His highness also requests that you wear this." She added while leaning back to the table that held the breakfast tray and grabbed a little box, handing it to Belle. Belle wrinkled her brow and opened the box, and damn near launched it across the room. She pulled the necklace from the box and dropped the box to the table, dangling the glittering silver chain in her fingers while inspecting the charm that dangled. It was a small silver key, a dark blue gem at the center of it, covered in insanely thin wire of silver, caging the gem into the key.

"Absolute jackass..." She muttered before stepping up to the mirror, weaving the silver chain into the bottom rungs of the corset so that the key dangled at her hip. "Let's go fight a prince, Sadie." Sadie visibly flinched, whether from the words themselves or the stabbing tone that they carried, Belle wasn't sure.

Davion turned when he heard Sadie and Belle coming up the stairs to the top of the tower, eyes instantly falling to Belle's empty neck. He lifted a brow, "Do your people not wear necklaces?" He offered as he motioned to the key cleverly woven into her corset strings.

"There is a difference between a necklace... and a collar." She offered casually while coming to a stop in front of Davion. Sadie gave a little curtsey and hurried back down the stairs, not wanting to be a witness to whatever was about to happen.

"I assumed you knew by now..." He crossed his arms over his chest, "You are mine. I can have the necklace reworked into a proper collar if you would like..." He tilted his head up slightly, looking down at her.

"We're choosing violence today, I see..." Belle mirrored his stance, arms crossing. "If it's tongue lashings you want, I'll have you flat on your back by the first round, mama's boy." She tipped her head toward the open room. "Shall we?" She flicked the key between her fingers and grinned as Davion blinked, caught off guard by her boldness. "After you train me to properly use my powers... You and I will be having a very serious talk, understand?" He wrinkled his brow, confused by the attitude and tone, before slowly nodding.

The training chamber was silent as Belle crossed the room, taking in the flickering candlelight and a thick layer of magic. Every inch of the stone walls shimmered faintly with runes etched in blackened silver, containment wards, old and dangerous. The kind of spells used to keep frenzied fae from unraveling the seams of reality.

Belle stood at the center of the room, barefoot, her arms crossed tightly over her chest. Her skin prickled from nerves, not cold. Davion stood a few paces away, the sleeves of his black tunic rolled to his elbows, shadows curling faintly at his fingers. His voice was steady. Measured. But low. Too low. "This room will absorb any power you lose control of," he said. "Nothing you do can escape it. Think of it like the warded area from the party. Just... stronger."

Belle nodded stiffly, scoffing. "And you just want me to... what? Seduce the air?"

He arched his brow. "Seduction is a weapon. But it's not the only one you have. I want you to reach. Not toward lust, but toward need. Your body knows the difference. So does your power."

She gave him a look, eyes shifting around for a moment, trying to fully grasp his meaning. "You're saying I should want to feed without wanting to fuck."

"Exactly," he said, and stepped closer. "You need to understand what your power is asking for. Hunger will always be there. This is about learning to answer it without losing yourself. Your feeding isn't for a life force, it isn't sustaining your ability to be alive; it should feel invigorating, it should heighten your senses."

"Great, so I'm a drug addict now." She rolled her eyes before forcing herself to be serious. Belle took a deep breath and closed her eyes, trying to feel the warmth at her core, at the base of her sternum. The glow that pulsed when someone looked at her too long, or when lips brushed skin. She let it swell in her chest, burn down her arms, and pool in her palms.

71

When Belle's power began to swell, Davion could feel it. The air grew thick. His heart rate shifted. He inhaled slowly, deliberately. "Now look at me," he gently commanded. When her eyes opened, the light honey brown color glowed; it was a faint golden hue, and it made Davion's heart stutter.

"I want you to take just enough to feel it, feel the charge," he murmured. "Not to feed, not to drain. Just to reach. If you can't stop, I'll pull you back." He stood about a foot from her, holding his hand out to her as an offering.

Belle hesitated, finally breaking the link and looking away from his storm gray eyes. "Why you?"

"Because I've already tasted it," he said, voice sharp and soft all at once. Davion would never admit it out loud, but he was dying to taste it again. "And I'm still standing." That answer shouldn't have made her pulse spike. But it did. Belle reached out, brushing her fingers against his wrist. Heat flared. Her power surged forward, wrapping around him like a velvet chain. Davion's breath hitched, but he didn't move. Didn't flinch. The magic of his smoke at his feet curled like dogs trying not to bark.

Belle felt it; the way his desire flared, how his mind resisted it while his body craved it. She drank a little of that heat, not enough to take, just enough to taste. She closed her eyes, savoring the thrum of it, the raw thread of want.

Davion stepped forward instinctively, almost against his will. "Belle," he growled low. She snapped her hand away like something had just burned her. The light in her eyes dimmed, the glow fading quickly. Her body trembled; it wasn't from weakness, though. It almost felt like a small jolt of adrenaline. Belle itched to move, to run, to do something to expel the energy. He stared at her, chest rising and falling, jaw tight. "You stopped," he said, quietly.

"I didn't want to lose control," she whispered to him. There was no sass in her tone, no attitude per usual, and despite the buzz humming through her veins, she had to admit to herself that it scared her.

"You didn't." He took another breath, placing his hand over the spot on his wrist that she had barely touched. "But next time... take a little more."

72

She tilted her head, half defiant, half afraid. "You sure you can handle it, princeling?" Belle bit down on her cheek, hiding the smile that threatened to bloom.

His smile was slow, almost dangerous. "We'll find out." He motioned her forward, trying to mentally settle his mind, knowing what was coming next.

Belle closed the distance between them, pressing her hand to his chest, spreading her fingers as her magic surged. It was no longer a gentle reach; it was a pull. Deep and instinctive. It wasn't lust that spilled into her in response; it was craving, sharp and visceral. She didn't just feel his desire; she drank it in. Power, dark and ancient, sank into her bones, licked across her nerves like lightning. It was filling her body with something that she never knew she was missing. Belle inhaled and tilted her head back, absorbing everything that Davion was giving her.

Davion... groaned. Low. Guttural. Like the sound was torn from his soul. His hands clenched into fists at his sides. His knees buckled before he could stop them, one crashing to the stone floor as he caught himself. Belle lowered herself with him, as if she had sensed that he was going to drop. She squatted in front of him, gently rubbing her thumb while her hand remained on his chest, as if soothing the ache away from him, as if the succubus in her was keeping him calm while she pulled everything from him.

Belle's lips parted, breath hitching. Her pupils dilated, overpowering the golden glow as the energy crackled through her, setting every nerve alight. Her spine arched. Her moan wasn't deliberate, but it was inevitable. It felt good. Too good. Too right. Too much. It wasn't just an adrenaline spike; it was clarity, it was joy, revelry, every good and right thing in the world.

Still, she pulled from him, pressing her hand harder against his chest, as need overcame her own senses. "Belle," Davion gasped, his voice hoarse, strained. He reached for her, meaning to push her away, but his hand curled around her hip instead, fingers digging in, slowly easing her closer to him. His shadows writhed around them both now, out of sync with him, slashing against the warded stone like they were trying to claw through it.

"Just a little more," she practically moaned, and gods help him, he leaned into her. The connection snapped into something deeper. The golden glow in her eyes flared around her blown pupils. His pulse faltered. His breath caught. Her body sang.

Davion collapsed. His entire body lay splayed out on the floor in front of Belle, drenched in sweat. Belle blinked out of the haze like someone had doused her in ice water. She tipped back, the magic ripping from her like a cord cut too fast, landing on her ass in front of him.

"Davion..." Her voice was high, panicked. "Shit... are you..." She crawled across the stone floor, closing the distance between them. He coughed once, shadows coiling protectively around him, his eyes glassy but locked on her.

"I told you... to take more," he rasped. "Not to take everything."

"I didn't mean to..." She hovered over him, unsure whether to touch him or not. Her hands were shaking with the panic that tore through her body, and her entire body buzzed with the surge still rippling through her. Her lips still tingled with power. "I couldn't stop."

"You have to stop," he snarled, finally lifting his head. "Or next time, it'll be someone who can't survive it." She swallowed hard.

"I thought you were strong enough," she whispered, looking away from him, down to her hands, wounded by the sting in his words even though she knew he was right.

He stared at her blazing, with power, yet half-broken, beautiful. "I am," he said, dragging himself up onto one knee. "But you brought me to my fucking knees with a touch, Belle." A beat of silence extended between them.

He stood slowly, unsteady, but still towering over her as she sat on her knees in front of him, and even now his body fucking ached for her. The power may have been buzzing through Belle, but the desire, the want, the sheer primal need for Belle wracked through Davion stronger than anything he ever felt or ever thought he would feel. And he said the one thing she didn't expect, "Next time... if you're going to go that far, you may as well finish it."

Belle gaped at him. "What the fuck do you mean, finish it?" Her voice cracked, too loud in the stillness of the training room. "You would die, Davion." She scrambled to her feet, staring up at him, still hesitant to touch him.

He shifted to face her fully now, sweat still clinging to his temples, eyes storm-dark. "Maybe." Davion gave a little shrug

She stared, frozen for a moment. "That's not a maybe kind of thing! That's a definite kind of thing. I saw the mage. I saw you... your..." She couldn't even bring herself to voice the way something cracked in her when she saw him lying on the ground in front of her.

"You didn't kill me," he said, voice low. "And you could have."

"That's not the point!" Her hands were clenched into fists, still trembling from the aftershock. "You told me to take more, and I did, and you collapsed. You're barely standing. If I hadn't stopped, your heart could've... I don't know... exploded or something." Her throat tightened. "I could've burned you from the inside out."

He took a slow step forward, the wards on the walls still humming faintly in the aftermath, as if absorbing whatever Belle hadn't, even pulling it back down to calm her. "I've trained with blades since I could walk," he said. "I've faced monsters, assassins, wild magic that eats minds for sport. But you..." He stopped in front of her, just close enough for her to feel his heat again. Davion shook his head slightly, a partially open-mouthed grin dancing at his lips. "You are the only thing that's ever brought me to my knees, and you weren't even holding a blade."

Belle blinked. "That's not a compliment." She shook her head before tossing her hands up in defeat.

"No," he said softly. "It's a warning. And a promise." Her breath caught. "Because if I'm going to teach you how to live with this, Belle... then I need to understand what it does to me. I need to stand in the center of the fire and not let it consume me."

She shook her head again, voice breaking. "You're not a test subject." She wrinkled her brow, trying to figure out just what the hell he felt he had to prove.

"No. I'm your anchor," he said. "I'm the one who will stand toe-to-toe with you and survive it. And if you don't learn that kind of control now, well then..."

"I'll kill someone who can't," she whispered. Davion didn't nod, didn't blink. Just met her eyes with all the terrifying, beautiful intensity he had.

"I want you," he said, so quiet it was almost a confession. "But not as a puppet pulled by magic. I want to want you, but on my terms. I want to beat it."

"And if you can't?"

His voice was dark silk. "Then I burn, and you will look ravishing in a crown..."

Chapter 10

The next few days were exhausting. Davion kept Belle moving from one task to the next as if he were terrified that the silence would eat her alive. Maybe somewhere in his mind, he knew that if she stopped long enough to breathe, she might start to come to her senses... But really, what senses would they be?

Belle began to wake before the sun just to reclaim a sliver of herself. Those quiet minutes belonged to Donovan and to the version of Belle who still wasn't sure what the hell was going on. She would allow herself to curl into one of the armchairs, clutching a pillow to her chest like it was a shield, and stare into the fading embers of the fire. Some mornings, the memories were gentle, filled with laughter and the way that his smile had always found her first. Other mornings, grief hit like a blade to the ribs, sharp and ugly and impossible for her to ignore. She didn't know what she was supposed to be now: a lover, a weapon, a prisoner? Donovan was gone, and nothing had shown up to replace him, not truly. He had guided her through so many things in life that, in his absence, Belle found herself more lost than ever before.

She learned to fold her grief away like a secret. In the silence, she let herself break, tears soaking into the pillow she held like it could hold her back. But the moment footsteps echoed outside her door, she stitched herself back together. Chin up. Smile sharp. No one here needed to know how close she was to falling apart. Belle would rather bleed in private than be seen as weak.

Once Sadie and Maude arrived, the day became a cacophony of noise. Davion trained her relentlessly, teaching her how to draw from the life force without bringing him to the brink of death, how to use her ability to make his will bend to her own, and even how to fight without relying on her powers. Over and over again, as if Davion felt that Belle would be going to war. Sometimes training devolved into teeth, nails, and friction. Belle quickly learned to get her revenge by cheating, pushing lust into him mid-spar, and Davion, never one to back down, met her halfway. Their sex was always rough, brutal even, a war they both kept choosing, and one Belle found far more satisfying than any practice blade.

There had been one time they were training with practice swords, and Belle had ducked under Davion's arm as he led a charge at her, the sword in his hand coming across fast. Switching her practice blade into her far hand, she trailed her fingertips at the back of his neck, just a simple, gentle graze, but it locked her powers in on him, and she watched as he slowed to a full stop. "Drop the sword." She whispered while slowing herself, stepping up behind him while the smoke swirled at his feet, almost rhythmically. She could see the internal struggle, the desire to please her after so many little touches throughout their session, overwhelming his desire to stay strong. When he did as he was told, Belle smiled, the sword clanging at the ground. "Turn to me." Almost robotically, Davion turned to Belle, fighting against her powers, which had only grown stronger, honed into the sharpest blade of them all. "Kiss me..." She whispered breathlessly, and he was on her, all but tackling Belle to the ground with the pure need that she was pumping into his body.

Belle moaned into it as she wrapped herself around him. Davion grunted after a moment and pushed himself away, leaving her on the ground while quickly standing and grabbing his blade, pointing it at her. "Cheater." He tried to stay serious, but there was a smile on his lips, and pride in his chest; this was exactly what Belle could be, temptress, and warrior all in one. There was pride for himself too, having learned the tell-tale signs of her power, feeling it in the air, and on his flesh like bubbles surrounding him; and how to deal with it, even when she forced such heavy waves onto him that he felt it would crush him, he couldn't breathe, he couldn't think, all he could do is want release. At the core of it, Belle was a creature of divine sensual nature; it was beautiful and maddening.

That night, he left her in her bed, her body blissfully sore from tangling in the sheets with Davion before giving her one more passionate kiss as he smoothed the hair from her face. It was rare that Davion stayed the night with Belle, but she never asked why. She assumed he had royal duties she had been pulling him from with their training sessions, or that he had to run away for the night, or they would have been long dead from exhaustion and dehydration; hours spent fucking on every surface in her quarters, hell, the entire castle.

Hours later, the door to Belle's quarters burst open, wood cracking as the guards in their blackened metal armor stormed into the room. Belle jolted up in her bed, holding the sheet to her naked body as her heart lurched into her throat. Before she could react, scream, or grab the blade that she kept tucked under her pillow, the guard's rough hands grabbed her and yanked her out of the bed.

The men were silent, minus their grunts from trying to prevent Belle from flailing. When she opened her mouth to scream, they shoved a gag in her mouth, tying it tightly around her head. Two men moved to the trunk at the end of the bed and grabbed a bundle of fabric, pale and shimmering, catching the moonlight as it pooled through the windows and sparkling an ethereal pale blue. The men pushed the fabric onto her body, tying the strings tight, snapping Belle's back straight before clapping iron-laden cuffs onto her wrists. The feeling of the metal bit into her skin. They were heavy, enchanted, thrumming with magic that stifled her own.

The moment the door was broken open, to the time the guards were literally hauling Belle from her chambers, had only felt like seconds. Such an abrupt entry, rude awakening, and harsh exit. She dug her heels in when her feet hit the ground, fighting against them, screaming into the fabric that muffled her sounds. They carried her through the castle and out onto the back terrace, where Belle had her first encounter with Queen Martine.

A velvet lined stage was set up at the top of the steps of the terrace overlooking the gardens and forest. Below the stage were crowds of people, royals and court members, joyfully mingling as Belle was hauled up onto the stand next to six other women, all wearing the same sheer gown as Belle, standing and smiling, waving flirtatiously at the men in the crowd. One guard stood behind Belle, his sharp blade pressed to her ribs, a silent threat: move and die.

The sudden commotion had Davion easing his way through the crowd. He had left Belle in her quarters; Sadie quietly left to guard Belle's door. He had left her safe, tucked away from this bullshit... But here she was, ceremonial gown and all, up on the dais, on display for hungry eyes. Her wide eyes locked onto Davion's as his feet started toward the dais.

"Ladies and gentlemen!" The Queen's fake honey-sweet voice boomed, and jovial music stopped; the crowd went silent, turning their attention to the Queen. Davion froze. Queen Martine lifted her hands in a grand sweeping gesture between the seven women on her right and the now eight men standing on her left. Davion had walked perfectly in line with the rest of the men, and now he had to play his part. "Tonight, we honor a tradition as old as the realm itself. Each woman stands here, a beacon of hope, a bearer of futures yet to be written." A soft murmur of appreciation rippled through the crowd. "For ages, the bloodlines forged on the night of The Hunt have ruled our kingdom and ruled it well." In all her grand motions, she stepped over to Davion, "And this year," Her voice swelled with mock pride, "We are graced with a most rare and honored participant." The crowd shifted, murmuring while turning toward Davion as the Queen's arm extended. "My dear son, our kingdom's strength and future, joins The Hunt tonight. To claim a wife, to create a future queen. To prove that loyalty and legacy are still the beating heart of Hightower." The crowd roared and applauded, and the women all but started drooling over the idea of the crown.

Davion remained frozen in place, even though he wanted to reach out to his mother and snap her neck right here and now, not caring that there were witnesses or the potential uprising her death would bring. The Queen was openly mocking Davion, forcing his hand into a situation that he had continued to avoid year after year, and using Belle as her fucking pawn... Davion was seeing red.

Martine stepped up to Davion, his hands flexed into tight fists at his side, as the Queen Mother leaned in and placed a kiss on his cheek. "Funny, isn't it?" She whispered, her breath a serpent's kiss against his ear. "All of your affection wasted on something so small... So beneath you... I wonder if you'll still want her... once there's nothing left to save." His hands twitched at the venom his mother whispered to him, itching for a blade or to call the black smoke to smother her very existence. She mocked him so openly, yet so privately... Small... Beneath him... As if Belle were a broken toy to discard. His vision narrowed, senses drowning out everything but Belle, the panic in her eyes, the gag in her mouth, her hands bound behind her back.

"This is a new low... even for you, mother..." He growled, doing his best to remain civil, remembering proper protocol and all the training he had growing up; he was the Prince, he couldn't lash out now, least of all against the Queen.

Turning back toward the crowd, Queen Martine flashed a smile, "And The Hunt begins!" She cheered, and a bell tolled. The barefoot women leapt off the stage, running while laughing, toward the woods beyond the castle. The guard at Belle's back shoved her forward, sending her stumbling from the platform. With a quick look over her shoulder, Belle glanced back at Davion as if to say, "Please find me," before she ran off with the other women.

As Belle stumbled and ran down the hill that led to the forest, Davion's eyes were locked on her, watching her like prey... like he was hunting her... He had to get to her first; he had to be the one to carry her back out of the forest. What a royal slap in the face that would be to his mother; not only would he get to keep Belle, the very person his mother was trying to dispose of, but she would now have the crown, as well. The other men down the line grew giddy, excited to chase down their future wives. Davion wanted to slaughter them all, let his smoke slink down their throats, and let them choke to death.

Deep in the woods, Belle's heart pounded in her head. Her lungs burned as she bit down on the gag, trying to gain traction, putting distance between herself and the men. She tripped over a root, and as she tried to right herself, she stumbled over a log and went down hard on the ground. She tumbled and rolled a few feet, grunting against the gag. Belle knew having her hands twisted behind her back slowed her down; being bound at all was keeping her from her freedom.

Another bell rang out, breaking the silence of the woods and the harsh, inhaled breaths Belle took. She scurried herself back against a tree, letting the rough bark dig into her arms. Grunting again, she shifted and lay back before lifting her hips, contorting her body, and ignoring the pain in her shoulders from the intense stretch while she eased her arms under her ass, under her legs and knees, and eventually curled her feet up, sliding them between her bound wrists. With another quick breath, she ripped the gag from her mouth, letting the fabric fall to the floor of the forest.

"I saw one!" One of the men yelled as he practically vaulted his way down the hill through the woods. Belle tucked the length of the translucent fabric up to her body, attempting to hide herself in the thick roots of the tree, holding her breath until the footsteps receded. Not too far in the distance, a loud pop echoed through the trees, and overhead, bright sparks threw light and distorted shadows over the forest; Belle could only assume that meant one of the women had been caught. If it were for a husband and a title, Belle didn't understand why they ran, why not just stand there to be caught.

Back on her feet, Belle continued to run, much easier now that her arms were in front of her, and not throwing her balance off as much. The woods seemed to stretch endlessly in every direction, twisted trees, sharp branches, and the cold soil under her feet. She leapt over a fallen tree, the thin glowing fabric of the dress catching and tearing, leaving tiny pieces of fabric attached to the bark. She held her arms over her face as she barreled through the brush, letting her hands take the brunt of the thorns and stickers.

When the second bell rang, Davion took off. Heavy, long strides carried him through the woods as he sprinted in the direction Belle had gone. He slipped through the trees like a living shadow. Silent, merciless eyes searching for only one person, his mind repeating that he had to find her, had to save her, he had to get to her first.

Sprinting through a tangle of brush, Belle let out a little scream as the ground fell out from under her. A hidden ledge on the other side of the brush, only six feet or so down, caught Belle off guard. Landing hard, pain lanced through her ankle as it twisted beneath her. Grunting through the pain, she tried to keep moving, but her pace had become a desperate hobble.

Davion had heard the sharp, quick squeal, and he knew in his gut it was Belle. He adjusted his direction, continuing his quick and deadly momentum while he tried to get to her.

"Mine!" A rough voice yelled out before tackling Belle to the ground, pinning her under him. He let out a sinister laugh as he held Belle down by her shoulders, straddling her and looking down at his prize. "Oh... The bound one." Another laugh rumbled from his mouth. "Did she bind you because you are just too wild to be tamed?" Belle bucked her hips, her heels digging into the dirt while she tried to reach out to the man in blind panic, aiming to hurt him any way that she could. The more she struggled, the harder he pressed his weight down onto Belle, grinding his hips into hers, and Belle could feel it, the disgusting, unmistakable pressure of something hard against her pelvis; her stomach twisted in revulsion.

She lashed out, snarling against her rising terror, her bound hands swinging wildly, catching him in the chin with a sharp, desperate blow. The sweaty man grunted, his head snapping back for a second, just enough. Belle jerked her knee up hard, aiming for the most vulnerable point she could reach. The man howled and twisted sideways, grabbing at his groin while cursing her. Belle rolled her hips, heaving the man off her body before scrambling up to her feet.

He caught her by her hair, wild, tangled, and free. "No!" she snarled, twisting against the pull, digging her nails hard into the dirt as if the traction would help her get away. Her nails scraped against something hard, a rock. Without thinking, without hesitating, Belle twisted her body with the rock in her hands. The rock slammed into the man's head, and his body fell... But that wasn't enough for Belle, even as the ground turned red. She knelt next to him and slammed the rock down on his face again, and again.

On the third downswing, Belle froze in place, arms still above her head as she dropped the stone. A brutal spike of

83

pain pierced through her heart, white-hot and merciless. She curled in on herself, gripping her bound hands on her chest, clawing as if she could make the pain stop by removing whatever the hell was stabbing her. Tears streamed down her face as she gasped for air. She didn't even realize that she had been screaming until her throat burned from the effort. Had she been screaming the whole time? When did it start? When did the pain end?

He had already torn through half a dozen false trails, passing half-glimpses of white gowns disappearing between the trees, but none of them was Belle. He slowed, needing to focus before he sailed off the edge of reason. And then he heard it. The scream. Raw. Broken. Tearing through the night like a blade.

Davion froze for half a heartbeat, every muscle in his body locking down hard enough to make his bones ache. "Belle..." He whispered her name as if the sound would carry him to her. There was no mistaking the voice. Hell, even if he hadn't known it was her voice, he knew there would be no other reason for that type of scream. It wasn't the coy laughter of the willing women playing their part. It wasn't the playful shrieks of a staged chase. No. This was terror. This was pain. His heart slammed against his ribs so hard he could taste blood. And then he was moving, running faster than he thought he could, his entire body screaming as the world narrowed to a single thread pulling him forward. Branches tore at him, roots snapped under his feet, and Davion didn't feel any of it. All he could feel was the desperate need to find her.

The scream died as he barreled through the undergrowth, replaced by a chilling silence that made the blood roar in his ears even louder. His stormy eyes searched the little clearing wildly, desperate to even lay eyes on her, but even now it was too quiet... Was he too late?

Something shifted to the right of him, branches cracked and bent, and a dark, armored man came charging into the clearing. Davion's eyes shifted, following the guard's trajectory, seeing Belle on the ground. Belle heard the noise too and shifted from where she sat, the bottom half of her dress stained red from the man's blood, the white fabric dimly glowing, covered in dirt. The scream was a splinter. The splinter that

84

stained your heart a little darker each time you took a life in this world.

Her eyes shifted to Davion, and she began to push up from the dirt and blood, reaching for Davion, and his feet were moving forward once more.

But...

He was too late, the charging guard crashed into Belle like a hammer, wrapping his arms tightly around her as their bodies rolled in the dirt, her reaching hand vanished in a flurry of delicate fabric and black metal; and with a quick, sickening snap, they vanished.

"No, no, no, no no..." his hands trembled as he ran to where Belle had been, falling to his knees, hands scrubbing roughly at the dirt. He needed something, anything, a sign of what kind of magic that was, which guard it was, anything that would tell him where Belle had been taken.

Freezing in place on his hands and knees in the blood-soaked dirt, Davion felt it. Something that felt like a thin thread of a bond that linked Belle to him from their last training. The whisper of her that had him knowing everything about her when she was close. It snapped. The invisible fiber that tied them together was pulled too tight; she was pulled too far, and it snapped. The pain of it ripped through his chest like a blade. Not the same as a splinter, not the stabbing pain that came from a kill, but more like a shatter, like pieces of him fell apart from the inside out.

Remaining on his hands and knees, he curled his hands into tight fists as he closed his eyes tightly; for a moment, the pain was too much for Davion to even breathe. He ground his teeth, swallowing the raw scream that threatened to break free. His mother did this; his mother caused this heartbreak on purpose.

He forced himself up, entire body trembling, hands covered in the blood of Belle's first kill; a stain he would carry for both of them now. His heart was hollow, crumbling from the inside, but his rage, his rage was alive, and it burned, forging those crumbled pieces into something hard and resolute.

"Courtland..." He muttered, and the small elf appeared next to him, "Summon my sister to my quarters..." His voice was low, almost gentle if not for the murderous thoughts that rolled through his mind. Davion started back toward the castle as Courtland vanished with a silent nod. He would walk back to the castle, come back to the joyous crowd empty-handed, smeared with blood and searing with rage.

Coming through the clearing back to the crowd, Davion locked eyes with his mother and gave her absolutely nothing. No sadness, no rage, no emotion. He simply stared at her as he climbed the steps, hushed whispers surrounding him, questions of blood, and Davion having not claimed a maiden. Stepping past his mother, he still said nothing and only turned his head to look at her until his neck couldn't turn anymore. Snapping his eyes forward, he went inside without a word. As much as he would have loved to reach out and strangle Queen Martine until her last breath left her wretched lungs, Belle was his priority, and he *would* get her back.

Chapter 11

The feeling of rolling from the tackle continued as Belle's surroundings swirled and warped. The world tipped sideways, the colors around her bleeding into streaks. Her stomach lurched as if she had fallen and then continued to fall. The pounding in her ears drowned out every other sound. The air shifted, growing increasingly colder by the second.

The breath she had already struggled to take became scarce, each inhale like pulling knives into her lungs. Her eyes frantically scrambled to lock onto anything that would explain just what the hell was happening. The portal spat her out like garbage. Belle hit the frozen ground hard, her shoulder slamming into ice that cracked but didn't break. The guard rolled off her and righted himself, standing up like nothing had happened. As he adjusted his armor briefly, the sound of metal scraping against metal clawed at the silence between them before he hauled Belle up off the ground unceremoniously.

The wind was vicious, a thousand invisible needles, stabbing into her exposed skin. It howled through jagged ice spires with a sound like the screams of the damned. Her teeth clattered in her skull. The cold carried a metallic tang, like blood or iron. Belle gasped, instinctively curling inward, but the shackles yanked taut, biting into her wrists. What little remained of the ceremonial dress clung to her in soaked, stained tatters, translucent under the brutal glare of the frozen sun, leaving her exposed under the guards' eyes.

The guards didn't say a word. They simply yanked her upright by her arms and dragged her toward the towering wall of ice ahead of a cathedral that rose like a blade out of the tundra, shimmering and merciless.

Belle stumbled once, twice, her bare feet stinging in the snow and ice; no one slowed for her, no one cared. The world here was cold. Hard. Beautiful in the way the stillness of a corpse might be.

As the doors to the Ice Cathedral yawned open with a low, shuddering moan, Belle knew, without magic, without words, this place had been built to erase people like her.

The guards themselves didn't cross the threshold of the giant doors; instead, they threw Belle forward, shoving her through the gates. She slid across the ground, her feet coming out from under her, and the same damned shoulder smashed into the ground again. The pain was quickly muted by the sudden pain in her gut.

Magic tore through her, like a knife made of fire and glass, lancing straight through. She screamed, crumpling on the ground as the magic twisted inside her, seizing something deep, something sacred, and ripped it out of her. This wasn't just physical pain; this was loss. Something had been taken. Something Belle didn't even realize was possible until it was gone. The guards lingered outside the gate, watching dispassionately as Belle convulsed, clutching at her abdomen, gasping for air. The threshold belonged to The Cathedral, and it demanded a sacrifice for entry. The magic ripping through her body hummed, sounding like someone mocking her, laughing at her. Belle opened her tear-soaked eyes to see the gates closing, sealing her into this frozen tomb.

She began to crawl across the floor, a slow, painful, jerking motion as her body all but convulsed in the quiet hope of any form of comfort or warmth. Her eyes were full of tears and trained on the large doors, and part of Belle genuinely wondered if she reached them, would she have the strength to push them open... Even if she made it out, where would she go? How would she survive in this flimsy excuse of a dress in the harsh snow and bitter cold? As the cursed pain started to fade and the tears threatened to freeze on her cheeks, Belle was yanked up from the ground once more. Two tall guards with wide shoulders, covered in layers of white leather and fur, pulled her clear off the floor; her feet didn't even touch the ice-covered stone as they dragged her through the hall. They led her to a dark, thin, winding staircase that twisted its way into the lower bowels of The Cathedral. She stumbled even now on the cold steps, one guard now in front and the other behind, as if anyone who had just suffered the shock and terror she had would be capable of fighting or even had a hope of doing so.

They shoved her forward once more, actions just as cold as their surroundings, and Belle stumbled into a cage. One of many, more than she could even dream of counting. A thin mattress on the floor, with pitiful scraps of fabric that were meant to cover her, to keep her just warm enough to keep her alive. Belle instinctively stepped onto the mattress, somewhere that would not have the frozen sting of the stone floor, and looked around.

A jail. A prison. A tomb. Someone had made sure to shove Belle away from anything that she had started to grow familiar with. Davion wouldn't... She thought to herself while her tangled hair whipped at her cheek when she spun to the side to look around.

The walls were lined with bodies, frozen mid-scream. Their eyes wide, mouths open, skin glazed with frost. One figure was smaller than the rest, a child, hand still pressed through the bars as though reaching for someone who never came. Belle's throat tightened. Those poor lost souls were left as a warning for anyone who would dare step out of line in this frozen hell.

She wanted to cry. She wanted nothing more than to just curl up and let the tears fall. Belle thought things couldn't get worse; being involved in The Hunt at the demand of the bitch Queen herself, but now... Belle allowed herself to sigh, her whole body shaking with the cold that sank into every inch of her. Watching the ghost of her breath, she sank to the floor, curling up as tight as her body could get, huddling around herself for warmth.

Throwing her head back, she screamed, "Ask that fucking bitch why not just kill me?" Not caring if a guard heard her, or even if the Queen herself would hear Belle. In the distance, Belle could hear faint rattling in other cages, a quiet reminder that Belle was not entirely alone.

"I'm sure we will get that order soon enough..." The voice rang like a half-forgotten song, eating at a memory, and Belle froze.

Belle wrinkled her brow, eyes shifting rapidly as she tried to place the voice she was hearing. It rang in her ears and tickled a memory, long buried. "When I talked you into taking the job, I had no idea that you had fae blood." One singular person came into Belle's view, in white robes from head to toe, but no distinct white faceless mask to hide their anonymity.

"Ivory." The name left her in a shocked exhale as she slowly rose from the cold floor, stumbling to the bars of her cage. "Ivory!" She reached for the frozen bars between the two of them, the chill biting at her fingers.

Even under the stark white robe, they were unmistakable. Skin dark and rich against the blinding cloth. The last time Belle had seen them had been in a back room over cheap whiskey, both grinning after a clean getaway. "How are you here?"

Ivory's dark eyes shifted from Belle to her outstretched hand, and they lifted a brow, shifting a shoulder away from Belle, avoiding touch. "We can end all of this suffering for you, Belle..." Their voice was low, coaxing. "You don't belong in a place like this." Ivory made a point of gesturing to the cage that separated the two. "You never did. You've always been a survivor. Let me do for you now what you've always done for yourself... I can get you out... I can take you home... You can survive..."

"How?" Belle asked, the singular word more of a breath than a sound.

Ivory's smile deepened, warm and poisonous. "Just talk to me, Belle..." They began, waving their arms in a grand circle, forming a chair on their side of the bars. "Tell me who you have met. What they have asked. Every detail that you can remember. I will pass it along, and the coldness will end." Belle's stomach dropped; they wanted information. Ivory gave Belle a slow, sickly sweet smile as they sat in the chair that they had conjured, folding one leg over the other, sending the white fabrics cascading across their form.

Belle's gaze shifted, hardened, and the warmth in her chest iced over. "You almost had me, Ivory..." Belle straightened her spine, standing tall while locking her honey brown eyes to Ivory's black ones. "Do you forget that I lied professionally when we met?" Belle shook her head, "I can also spot a liar a mile away... Ivory..." Belle used their name pointedly, calling them the liar without using the words herself.

There was a new stab of betrayal that slowly leaked its way through Belle. Ivory had been trusted by Belle; they had been friends, or at least that is what Belle thought. Perhaps she was meant to be a pawn to Ivory the entire time.

Ivory's smile twitched, a small, infuriating little curve that Belle wanted to slap off their face, nodding while adjusting their hands in their lap. "What magic did the Hightower boy unlock in you?" They asked while tilting their head off to the side. "We could provide better than the life you had back in your realm, Belle..." Ivory inhaled a dramatic breath while leaning back for a moment before leveling with Belle. "The Holy Land could guide you to the crown, Belle. Wouldn't that be divine? You would have magic, power, and title, you would never want another thing because between ruling Hightower and working with us, anything you could ever imagine would be given to you..." They spoke with their hands, as they had always done, but now when their hands flourished, small sparks flew from one hand for the dramatic, while snowflakes fell from the other.

Belle recognized the manipulation as each word spilled from Ivory's mouth, and part of her heart cracked, shattered, even. She thought that she could trust Ivory; they had worked together so many times. Ivory had been there for Belle when no one else was... But now this... Belle physically brought her hand to her chest, wincing as she rubbed the tips of her fingers in small circles over her heart, the betrayal sinking into her core before dissolving into something else entirely. "How are you able to travel between realms?" Belle asked quietly, turning the pain of betrayal into power, something Belle excelled at. "How are you here?!" Belle shouted while leaning closer to the bars of her cage, "There are no more keys, there is no way back to our world. So, how are you here?" Ivory began to smile, all too slowly; it made Belle feel uneasy.

"So you know about the keys... And what they do..." Ivory nodded slowly, eyes shifting off into the distance as if they were thinking. "Belle, keys aren't the only way of travel..." Ivory offered with a half shrug, pursing their lips momentarily, considering their words carefully. "Keys were just the vessel. The power has always been there... It just needs to..." They shifted their eyes, pausing as if looking for their words, "Grow... Be fed..." Ivory extended a gloved hand toward Belle in her cell, knowing that the iron cuffs on Belle's wrist rendered her less than a threat. Belle hated the way that it sounded, as if magic was the only living thing that they understood. "Though, none of that would be your concern... Your proposed role is much different. Just bring the Hightower boy to kneel..."

Davion... They saw Davion as a threat... Belle's jaw ticked as she tried to untangle the web that she found herself in. They had people in the castle. They had ways of walking through the realms that did not require the keys. They had the Queen. But Ivory was sent to get The Holy Land the future King... Belle straightened her spine, tilted her chin up slightly.

"You cannot honestly give that boy such devotion, Belle... Did he not have Donovan killed?" Ivory stood from her chair, and it fell to the ground in snowflakes. "Has he not kept you prisoner in the walls of the castle and only fed you the information that he felt you needed?" They stepped closer to the bars, lowering their voice. "The Belle that I've known would want revenge for that... Payback for hurting Donovan..." There was an edge to their voice, a challenge to their words, baiting Belle.

"Fuck off, Ivory." Belle shifted on the small pad on the ground, shifting her gaze away from Ivory. "Better believe I will kill you when I get the chance. Mini heart attack from killing someone, be damned." She rolled her eyes and shrugged before waving a dismissive hand at Ivory.

"The Holy Land will only wait for so long before it decides they have no use for you. And then you will just be another force to feed the machine... Another nothing... Another death." Ivory stepped past Belle's cage, and Belle watched through narrowed eyes as Ivory left; the only noise now was the sound of Ivory's shoes on the cold stone and the wind as it whispered its way through the cathedral.

Chapter 12

Khandra stood near the hearth in her brother's private war room, the fire spitting low embers into the silence. Her arms were crossed tight over her chest, posture rigid, poised like a weapon waiting to be drawn. She'd been summoned without explanation, only a single sentence from Courtland, "Your brother needs you, now." His face had been pale, eyes darting like he had wanted to say more, but didn't dare. Khandra's hand was extended to him before he could finish the sentence, and he pulled her through the elven way of transportation, like a portal, but much more silent, gentler.

Now she waited. No fae wine in hand. No quips to break the ice. Just silence and the sound of her bare feet padding back and forth across the worn carpet, and the weight of dread coiling in. Khandra hugged herself, nails digging into her ribs, her mind racing ahead of the moment as if trying to catch up to something it should have already seen. How could she not have known something would happen, how could she not have seen it? The door creaked open behind her.

Davion entered, silent, sharp, barely restrained. His movements were precise, controlled in the way only people who were seconds away from breaking moved. A smear of dried blood darkened his collar, and his right hand flexed once, smoke twitching at his fingertips before curling away. He was far more disheveled than Khandra could ever recall seeing him. His short hair was thrown all over, jaw tensed, refusing to release. His eyes were somehow both blank and full of rage just the same. He was covered in dirt, sweat, and blood, and as he shifted his gaze to Khandra, he looked like he was ready to start a war.

Khandra straightened immediately, eyes narrowing. She didn't speak. She didn't have to. He stared at her from across the room, the space between them warping under the tension, thick with unspoken rage. His magic flickered across the floor, restless, small plumes of smoke curling across the floor before puffing out. The flames behind her flared and dimmed, responding to the storm in him.

When he finally spoke, his voice came low and strained, like each word scarred his throat on the way out. "Belle is gone." A beat of silence held between them as Davion forced a steady breath. "And our mother..." He didn't finish. He didn't need to. Khandra's stomach dropped.

The way he said those words. It wasn't political. It wasn't about leverage or strategy. Their mother had made it personal. Khandra inhaled through her nose, slow and controlled, but her heart was a drum in her chest. She'd teased him about Belle. Mocked the softness she brought out in him in the way that a sibling would and should. But now... Khandra saw it for what it truly was. This wasn't just another entanglement. Belle had carved herself into him, and it had nothing to do with her being a succubus; this wasn't Belle's magic tangling itself in his veins. This was real and true, and for a moment, Khandra grieved silently with Davion.

"What do you need from me?" Khandra asked, voice even, despite the dread spearing through her chest.

Davion gave a soundless laugh, nothing more than a twitch at the corner of his mouth and a sharp, short exhale. It wasn't a smile. It was something darker. His well practiced mask was cracking at the edges. He crossed the room in three slow, tense steps. Towering. Coiled. His jaw worked as if he couldn't decide whether to scream or collapse. "Everything." His tone screamed all the emotions that he wouldn't allow himself to. Khandra didn't flinch. "You can move freely where I am chained by duty. I want her back, Khandra." His voice cracked slightly, but it felt like the sound of a wall giving way under pressure. "I need her back." He looked away from Khandra, and she watched as his shoulders sagged under the weight of his admission.

There it was. Not a command. Not a royal decree. But a plea. His eyes, usually cold, calculating, unreadable, were raw. Every emotion he wouldn't allow himself to say was reflected in his stormy gray eyes. His shadows had stilled, like even the magic in him knew not to interrupt.

Khandra's breath hitched. A thousand replies rose in her throat. Sarcasm. Reassurance. Fury. But all of them fell away when she saw the way he looked at her, not as the Prince of Hightower, but as her brother. Wounded. Hollow. Yet still trying to pretend he wasn't. She reached up and cupped his cheek, grounding him in the only way she knew how. Her palm was warm, steady. "Leave it with me, brother," she said gently. "The next time you see me, I will have your woman." His eyes fluttered shut at her words; with a settled breath, he leaned into her hand, not fully, not desperately. Just enough to admit he was still human underneath all the magic, chains, and the rumbling volcano of emotions that was bound to erupt.

Khandra left without another word, the train of her dress trailing behind her like a shadow with purpose. The door clicked shut. The silence that followed wasn't calm. It was charged, dangerously electric, like a bright bolt of lightning ready to strike in the dead of night.

Davion stood frozen in place for exactly three seconds. Then he exhaled once, the breath trembling as he exhaled, and then he allowed his power to explode.

The smoke took form, solid and sharp like daggers as it lashed out across the room, like beasts loosed from their chains, ripping through furniture, clawing at stone walls, shattering the untouched wine bottles with a shriek of glass. The table cracked through the middle. A chair slammed into the far wall and splintered. His war maps fluttered from the desk and were immediately swallowed by chaos, parchment shredded and flying. The fire in the hearth flared to life again, taller than it should've been, casting warped light across Davion's features: sharp, furious, and grieving.

Davion stood in the center of it all, unmoving, breathing hard as if he'd just come off a battlefield. His shadows writhed around him, mirroring his fury like a second skin made of rage and regret. The destruction stuttered for a moment, like his grief had stolen the breath from his fury, and then it surged again. "She was mine," he growled, barely audible over the roaring flames and thrashing magic. "And I let her go. I wasn't fast enough." A goblet shattered against the wall. Another chair followed.

He dropped to his knees like his fury had ripped him hollow. Shadows pooled around him, curling tight, not in anger now, but in mourning. "I wasn't fast enough...." He repeated as the chaos around him settled, the smoke fizzled out, returning to its natural state.

In the silence, Davion pressed his bloodied hand to the stone floor and whispered, not a command, not a spell. Just one word, soft and raw, "Belle..."

Chapter 13

The cold had teeth, and it bit deep. Gnawing on bone and breath alike, sinking so far into Belle that she wondered if it would ever leave. Frost clung in delicate, mocking webs to her hair and lashes, glittering whenever she moved. She curled tighter into herself, tucking her raw, shackled wrists against her chest, trying to conserve what little body heat she had left. It didn't help. The icy wind howled straight through the jagged bars of her cage, bars that weren't metal or stone, but pure ice, slick and razor-sharp, glittering mockingly in the weak light of dawn. They hadn't even given her a proper cell. Just a cage, exposed, leaving her vulnerable and left to be forgotten.

She wore a thin shift; rough, scratchy, and barely thicker than a bed sheet. She had deconstructed the flimsy excuse for a bed and wrapped herself in the thicker of the two blankets, tucking her feet under herself; the slippers may as well have been stockings with how thin they were. Her "meal" had been a lump of cold bread no bigger than her palm, left on the ground where she had to crawl to reach it, her frozen fingers fumbling at the edges. She hadn't eaten all of it. Not yet. Some stubborn part of her, the part that still remembered who she was, had tucked half of it into the folds of her shift, hoarding it like a dragon might hoard treasure.

She knew deep in her battered, hollow bones; they weren't going to make this easy. They weren't trying to house her; they were trying to erase her. Judging entirely by the immeasurable number of faces frozen in the walls, this place would bring so much more than just the cold. Belle hadn't slept; she knew torture was coming.

Belle shifted, wincing as the frozen floor bit into her bare legs through the pitiful pad of an excuse for a mattress, and cracked her eyes open. The Cathedral stretched above her like a rib cage made of ice and cruelty, every surface gleaming blue and white under the watery morning sun. The ice groaned faintly overhead, and somewhere far off, a muffled cry carried through the hollow air before vanishing into silence.

Around her, she could see other people and creatures rotting away in their frozen cages, just like her. Miserable, alone, suffering, and the guards safely behind their faceless white masks, watching her from a distance as if she were a dangerous, filthy thing. As if she were the thing that infects this perfect, frozen world with her impurity. Belle shifted, pulling her knees up to her chest, pressing her clothed heels onto the ice while pressing her forehead to her knees; the thin shift fluttering around her in the frigid wind as she fought the rising tide of despair that gnawed at her mind.

She must have drifted off to sleep while curled in her cage; she didn't mean to, maybe it was hypothermia, and she would stay asleep forever. She couldn't be so lucky. "M'lady..." A male voice, quiet and gentle, coaxed her from her sleep. Belle barely moved, lifting her head slightly to look at the man who stood on the other side of the bars that held her in. "Good. You're alive." He shoved a blanket through the bars, tossing it as close to Belle as he could.

Slowly, weakly, she crawled to it and wrapped it tightly around herself. Belle didn't know this man, didn't know if he could be trusted, but she was going to take the damn blanket regardless; any hope of warmth was a blessing. "You smell like my sons." It was a simple sentence, but it rocked Belle's core, threw her off her axis, and made her sit upright even as she tried to hide her entire body in the little blanket.

"Excuse me?" She asked while shifting closer to the man. He had greying hair that once would have been full and dark, and a matching beard, if for nothing else than for warmth, but it was his eyes that caught Belle's attention. Storm grey, soft eyes. Such a contrast to their harsh environment. They were eyes she knew without knowing, eyes that had stared at her before, but now from another face. Belle narrowed her eyes, shaking her head a little. Davion had told her that his father was dead.

"Oh... This is a hallucination," she nodded to herself, trying to make sense of her situation.

Shaking his head, he reached his hands through the bars, motioning for Belle to place her hands in his. "I assure you, I am as real as you are." When their hands met, a familiar sensation took over. Once it had felt cold, relaxing, but now, here in the harsh cold tundra, what was cold felt warm; it was a relief, and Belle could have fallen apart. It was more than heat, it was a gentle slowing of the relentless ache in her bones, a stillness settling into her that made it easier to breathe. What it was, was Khandra's magic. The time magic Khandra used to heal wounds. Tears welled in her eyes as she bowed her head, thankful for the unusual warmth and the soothing of her aches and pains. "Which of my sons?" He asked gently, shifting from the squatting position he had been in to sitting on his knees in front of Belle. "Are they well? And what of Khandra? Is she safe?" Belle could see there were more questions he wanted to ask, but as his magic worked through her, making her feel a little more alive and aware, Belle had her own questions, too.

Belle stayed frozen, kneeling in the ice and filth, the tattered blanket clutched tight around her body. The man, this stranger, with the twins' storm-grey eyes, sat patiently on the other side of the bars, his hands still gently cupping hers through the freezing cage. Warmth pulsed into her. Not enough to erase the damage. Not enough to undo what had been taken.

But enough.

Enough to remind her she was still alive. Enough to remind her she could still fight. Belle squeezed his hands weakly, lifting her head to meet his gaze. "Who are you?" she rasped, her voice barely above a whisper.

The man smiled a soft, tired thing that didn't reach the corners of his eyes. "Once, I was a king," he said simply. "Now, I am just a father... trying to undo what he should never have allowed." Belle's heart hammered against her ribs, her mind racing through half-formed possibilities, memories, and questions.

He saw the doubt in her eyes. The mistrust. The fire, still smoldering, even as her body threatened to fail her. And he didn't get angry. He didn't push. He only let go of her hands and sat back slightly, giving her space. "I can help you," he said softly, his breath misting in the cold air. "But only if you want me to. Only if you choose it."

Belle stared at him. Nobody here had given her a choice. Not the guards. Not the priests. Not the Cathedral itself. Certainly not the magic that had ripped through her when she crossed the threshold. Faces flashed in her mind, every one of them taking something from her without asking. The Queen's cruel smile. The guards' faceless stares. Davion's domineering ways. Now that a choice had been presented to her, she realized that she hadn't had a choice since she fell into this fucking world.

But now here, in this prison of ice, this frozen tomb, someone was offering her a choice. Small. Insignificant. But it belonged to her. Her throat burned as she swallowed hard, tears stinging her cracked lips, and slowly, painfully, Belle nodded.

The man smiled again, this time a little brighter, a little warmer, pleased to see that whichever of his boys had chosen her, had chosen a fighter. Without another word, he reached through the bars again and pressed something small and cold into her palm. It was smooth and heavy for its size, the surface black with faint natural striations. A stone; not magic, not cursed, just a stone. "You'll know what to do when the *time* comes." He rose to his feet, winking to Belle before nodding and walking away. Time, of course. Khandra had the gift of time, and she chose to use it to heal, but time, nonetheless. Davion would come for her, and the King had already seen it happen.

Chapter 14

Khandra had left the castle in the quiet of the night after The Hunt, the vow to her brother taken seriously. She couldn't believe their mother had stooped so low, but thankfully for Khandra, she knew exactly who to turn to. Khandra typically came across as another pretty face, a clueless spoiled princess in a world of court politics, but she always watched; she had always paid attention to them, and she quietly learned as much as she could. Moments like this were why, so that when the board shifted, she would already know her next three moves.

It had all left Davion with more questions than answers. Now, seeing just how ruthless his mother was, he began to question everything. Maybe Donovan had been right in stealing the key and leaving. Maybe his mother only ever had her best interests at heart, not the kingdom's. No, not his mother. He no longer saw Martine as his mother. Davion started to see his mother as a traitor, one wholly undeserving of the crown, abusive and reckless with her power. The more research he did while locked away in his tower, the more he began to see links between his mother's ideology and that of the Holy Land's. All these years following his mother, believing that what she had planned for the realm was in its best interest, constant research and progress toward being able to bring the stolen keys back for safekeeping. Yet it was Martine who wished to conquer and subjugate.

Davion had spent twenty years being told how awful his brother was, and that aside from having escaped with the Keys of the Realm, it was a blessing that he was likely dead in another realm. Twenty years of having his loyalty and obedience drilled deep into the core of his being; absolutely brainwashed by Martine.

The lies washed away in the moment that Martine had Belle brought to the dais the night of the hunt. The loyalty rinsed from Davion like dirt in the rain. Now he thirsted for the truth. He quested for a solution.

He made his appearances when his mother called or when he was required to be in court. He played the part of a devoted son, sad that his mother took away his favorite toy. He planned their next attacks, helped ensure their borders were safe, and helped look for the few remaining keys; all things he had done long before Belle had stepped into his world. He was biding his time, waiting for word from Khandra, or until his mother made yet another stabbing comment and he finally snapped.

Gossip rumbled around him as it always did; snippets of hushed conversation cutting the moment he entered a room, eyes following him in the reflection of gilded pillars. Whisperings in the court about how sad it was that he came out of The Hunt unmatched. People murmured about the Queen and her plans to match Davion with someone she saw fit to wear the crown. On one hand, if he killed her now, the crown would be his, as it was always intended to be; on the other, if he killed her now, Davion would never know just how far his mother's treachery went, and with his revelations came a deep sense of needing to know just how betrayed he really was.

"When will you be done pouting, Davion?" Queen Martine asked as she breezed into his private quarters, her presence making the air feel colder despite the fire burning in the hearth. She brought him back to reality instead of being lost in thought as he stared at the fire. "She was just one woman. You are the Prince of the Hightower Kingdom; you could have your pick of any woman." She lowered herself to the couch opposite Davion, hands folded neatly in her lap, eyes glittering with cold satisfaction. "Shall I gather them all and line them up? You can pick whichever you like, perhaps one that is..." She paused and smirked, "Subservient. I would also add disposable... but..." She made a small humming sound while shrugging her shoulders, signifying that Belle was nowhere to be found; and therefore, disposed of.

Davion's fists clenched against the arms of the chair, the tendons in his hands straining. The firelight danced across his face, hiding the fury building behind his calm exterior. With a slow, steady breath, he smiled, just a little, and angled toward the Queen. "Thank you, mother." His voice was smooth as glass. "Your concern for my happiness is... touching." He added a little subservient nod to appease her. Inside, his heart roared, and the walls of his loyalty to this vile, repulsive woman continued to crumble.

Her thin lips curled at his thanks; she knew it wasn't sincere, but she would take it, nonetheless. "You should be thanking me." She emphasized while standing. "I saved your future from weakness." She stood now, stopping behind his chair, her fingers grazing his shoulder. "Once you are properly matched with an appropriate mate," she murmured, "you will understand. Love is for the powerless. Legacy is for kings." She took a few steps toward the door before turning to face him once more. "She would have given you nothing." Her voice sharpened now, "No heirs, no alliances, no respect from the court. Only scandal and weakness." She scoffed, shaking her head before straightening her spine, when the only response she got from Davion was a slow nod. "You are my son. Not some lovesick fool clinging to broken things." As she approached the door, it opened for her, one of her private guards, the quiet one with the bright red hair, stood on the other side. "You are the Prince." She snapped at him, "Act like it." With that, she left him to his silence once more.

Only once he was certain the Queen was gone, Courtland materialized next to Davion. "I have news." He nodded, and Davion returned the motion, glancing over his shoulder to make sure the Queen didn't linger. "Khandra made contact," He kept his voice quiet, "She went to the Wildelands. His Royal Highness Kaelith has a guest who will aid Khandra in her quest." Courtland didn't need to voice it out loud; naming names and telling details was too dangerous. But Davion understood, and as much as he hated the option Khandra chose to save Belle, it was very clever on his little sister's part. Hope flickered, sharp and dark, in his chest. The Queen may have left the room believing she was the victor, but the game

103

was only beginning, and Davion would be the one to write the rules.

Chapter 15

Khandra hadn't risked the use of portals until she was a long way from Hightower Castle; for all Khandra knew, Martine had spies that would track her movements. She may seem like the happy-go-lucky carefree sibling of the three, but Khandra could be just as tactical, just as ruthless and cunning. Men always said women let their emotions get in the way; well, Khandra believed that women were emotional, yes, but that emotion could move mountains, reshape the realm itself, and she was on a fucking quest.

She had traveled nonstop through the night, and well into the morning, beyond when the sun was at its highest, before she felt she had gained enough distance to portal to the Wildelands. She shook her head slightly, rolling her shoulders and steadying her nerves before stepping through the portal. The air on the other side was warm, instantly so much warmer than back in Hightower. The castle loomed against the dusk like a black wound carved out of the night sky. Not wood, not just stone. Obsidian. Forged in fire. Generations before King Kaelith molded their kingdom. The dark glass drank in the last light of the sun and threw it back as a glinting promise of violence. Hightower built their walls so high to hide the lies and project a power of perfection. Obsera, the crowned capital of the Wildelands, wore their battles on their sleeves and declared their open truth so loud that all would know it.

Crossing the border through the obsidian gates, the air shifted. It thrummed, thick with heat, smoke, and the scent of scorched earth. The heartbeat of a city that did not pretend to be anything other than what it was. This city was alive in ways

Hightower had never been. Not polished in perfection, but beating and breathing in its flaws. Khandra hadn't made it too far into the heart of the city before a small, quick-footed elf appeared, her hair a wild mass of curls woven through with beads and scraps of colorful cloth. "Princess Khandra," she chimed, bowing, "Welcome home." Khandra blinked, momentarily thrown. Home? She had to admit she did spend a fair bit of time in the Wildelands; it was away from her mother, and King Kaelith made sure she was taken care of. "The King is expecting you." She motioned for Khandra to follow, "He said to bring you to him directly. No delays." And they were off, weaving through the city, up the obsidian casted stairs, straight through the front doors of the castle, and right into the throne room. Everything had passed by them in a blur. The little elf was on a mission, and she knew exactly what to do. She gave a quick bow to the king while clearing her throat, quietly announcing their arrival before vanishing in the same fashion Courtland often did.

"Princess Khandra Hightower." His voice boomed into the mostly empty throne room. Kaelith was not a small man by any means; Khandra estimated he was just a hair taller than her brothers, but his body sculpted for power gave her no doubt that in a hand-to-hand fight, Kaelith would wipe the floor with her brothers, potentially both at the same time. "Your quick and hushed arrival surely means you have come to collect our friend..." He closed the distance between himself and Khandra, and she did all she could not to lick her lips as she took in his physique; the blackened lines that swirled from his wrists to his shoulders, symbolizing the flame he carried, and the flame of his land.

"Indeed, your Majesty. Situations have shifted, and I require our friend to help rectify them." Kaelith's smile was slow and sharp, like a wolf scenting blood on the wind. "My brother and I continue to appreciate your hospitality, and if he has not done so himself, I would request aid from a small group of your men in our quest." His smile grew as he stepped closer to Khandra. In his kingdom, most flinched, most backed down when he approached so closely; but Khandra held her ground, only shifting the angle of her head, lifting her chin to meet him eye to eye.

106

"What will you offer in return for such a precious favor, Princess?" He asked while folding his arms over his chest, when he finally came to a stop a few feet from her; his eyes roaming over her body as she had known they were prone to do.

"Nothing you would not already take for yourself, should you find it to be worthy..." She retorted, words with multiple meanings, as they often bantered back and forth.

"Kaelith, please stop trying to fuck my sister with your eyes. I am certain whatever she is here for, it is more important than getting your dick wet." A lighter, much more cheerful voice came from the side of the room as footsteps echoed around the chamber.

Khandra exhaled through her nose, a long-suffering sigh that managed to be both exasperated and contain a sound of fondness. Without taking her eyes off Kaelith, who, to his credit, only looked mildly amused at the interruption, she lifted her hand and flipped Donovan off with an elegant, practiced flick of her fingers. "Wonderful," Khandra muttered. "Truly, brother, I have missed your charm."

Donovan grinned wider, the picture of smug innocence as he sauntered forward, boots tapping lightly against the black glass floors. The sound was sharp and hollow, each step echoing like a clock ticking down. Closer now, Khandra could see the shadows under his eyes, the lean frame, the barely healed scars peeking from beneath his rolled sleeves. It wasn't exactly that the Wildelands had been unkind to her brother; it was naturally rougher than Hightower, and, she imagined, the plush mortal realm he had been stowed away in. But the roughness of the Wildelands also did not break him. It would take a lot to break him... and unfortunately... Khandra was about to deal the first blow and prayed it wouldn't be his tipping point. "You didn't come all this way just to save me from a fiery political marriage, did you?" Donovan teased, ruffling his already messy hair.

Khandra shook her head, the sharp humor bleeding from her face like the last embers of a dying fire. She glanced at Kaelith, inhaling a steady breath as she tilted her chin up. "Permission to speak to my brother in private?" Khandra smiled at the king, a polite little dagger of a smile, and offered the faintest curtsey as she essentially dismissed the King from his own throne room.

Kaelith blinked, and for a moment, he simply admired this infuriating, stunning woman. There was a question in her tone... but the demand beneath it burned hotter. "Of course, my flame..." The word slid into place between them like a secret, and Kaelith's smile sharpened, knowing, warm, and a little wicked, before he turned on his heel and stepped away from the siblings. He pretended to study a tapestry at the far end of the hall depicting the creation of the Obsidian Castle, forefathers scorching sand into blackened glass. In truth, he couldn't recall a single stitched detail. He was far too busy thinking about Khandra. Tapestry be damned.

Khandra waited a beat, watching as the King strutted away and folded his arms over his broad chest. The skirts of her gown fluttered around her when she turned back to Donovan, grabbing his forearm to bring his attention back to her, not Kaelith as he gave them space. "It's Belle," she said, voice steady but low.

Donovan stilled. The slight color of red that he had already been seeing at the blatant flirtation between Kaelith and his baby sister was replaced by a cold chill that washed over him. "What about her?" he asked, tone dangerously flat. Khandra stepped closer, lowering her voice even further, the words pressing hard against her chest like iron bands. "Our mother staged The Hunt." She started, gently reaching out to take his hands into her own. "Belle was forced into it, bound and gagged. She had to fight... She had to kill..." Khandra took a breath, watching Donovan's mind begin to turn dark. "She was captured by the Queensguard and taken through a portal before Davion could reach her." She hesitated, looking down at their hands. "We believe she was taken to the Ice Cathedral in the Holy Land."

For a moment, the throne room was so silent that Khandra could hear the crackle of the far torches licking the obsidian walls. Donovan didn't move. Didn't breathe. And then he gently took his hands from Khandra's, slowly nodding, processing the hellacious news his sister had just delivered. "How long ago?" He asked roughly.

"Closing in on a week now. I had to be sure that our mother did not track me to get here. I could not risk bringing her to you." Her admission turned into a slight plea, begging forgiveness for her delay without asking. "Davion is still playing his part at court. I left the moment he told me. We need you, Donovan. We need your army. We need you to bring her home..."

Donovan grumbled under his breath, shaking his head slightly at the notion of home, it brought an ache he didn't bother hiding. "Guess it's a good thing I was already building a rebellion... Now we'll have a fucking war."

Kaelith rejoined the pair while letting out a hearty laugh, arms still folded as he watched the Hightower siblings with something dangerously close to pride. "In the land of ice, you will need fire to match its burn." He held his hands out to the side, inserting himself into the group, volunteering his services and his power for their mission, and making it abundantly obvious he heard every word. Khandra reached out and squeezed Donovan's shoulder once, hard.

"This isn't war... Not yet... This will have to be stealthy, Donovan. Mother must not get wind that this was us, not until we show up at the castle with Belle in hand." Ever the tactician, Donovan nodded at Khandra, knowing she was right.

Internally, Kaelith was thrilled to take his small group of Razhan, his most elite soldiers, into the Holy Land. Stealth mission or not, they would get to burn things, break things, hurt things, and that is what they lived for. "When do we leave for the Holy Land?" He asked excitedly while rocking on his feet.

"How soon can you be ready?" Donovan asked while flexing his hands into fists, his shadows twitching faintly as if they, too, wanted to tear a path through the snow and bring Belle home.

Chapter 16

Numb... Belle was so numb... The cold was relentless; it beat her down at every turn. Everything she touched, everywhere she looked, was more fucking cold. She opened her eyes slowly as she heard the gate creep open again. Every day now, they collected her from her cell. Every day, they tried purging her wickedness, pressing their magic and agenda upon her. Repeatedly, they told her how awful she had been and how the ice would cleanse her anew. They wanted her silent, compliant, and empty. Every time she felt herself slipping, giving in to what they wanted of her, she remembered the rock King Davion had given her, and remembered that he somehow saw a way out of this for her.

The first few days, she had cried to sleep, the warmth of the tears on her face quickly chilled and froze; and then tears did her no good. Nor did living on the memories of Donovan, Davion, or even Khandra. There was nothing good here; there was nothing to bring her anything but misery. She was starving, filthy, and she was withering away, both in body and spirit. When the guard stepped in through the open door, she offered her cuffed hands to him; at least they'd help her off the frozen ground, though it was anything but gentle. They ripped her up from the cold floor and pulled her along.

By now, they had started to repeat their *treatments*, as none of them had worked the first time. Though each wore her down, little by little, until they hoped one would finally work. By her estimation, it had been close to two weeks, if not a little more. What was the sense in staying on guard and wasting her energy counting the days she had been trapped in this frozen hell? There was no escape, no return to the safety of Davion; certainly no return to the jovial laugh of Donovan. She grumbled under her breath as the tears threatened to tear her apart again.

They hauled Belle to a square room, with a pillar of ice in the middle, and shackled her to it. The water would come soon. Water so cold it felt like it cut her a thousand times over, pelting her back, instantly soaking her to the core. Before the torture could start, Belle lowered herself to her knees. Half to make herself seem smaller, half because she genuinely did not have the strength to stand. She could hear the small incantation whispered, and she took a slow, painful breath in, knowing what came next.

On day one of their torture, she refused to scream, refused to give them the satisfaction of knowing they were getting to her. She gritted her teeth hard as the never-ending jets of water pelted her back, no doubt burrowing a few new holes into her piece of shit shirt. She didn't even have time to shiver; the water didn't come in a trickle, she was soaked before she could blink. The chants continued, the water continued. The chants stopped; the water stopped. One of their priests promised her such sweet things if she would just give in and repent for her wicked ways. Not one of them had tested her magic, not one of them knew what she was, or what she was capable of; none of them probably cared. They were set on turning her into another mindless follower before they would pretend to care. The chants started; the water started. The chants continued, the water continued. The cycle went on like this. Giving Belle only minutes to breathe the staggeringly sharp, cold air that burnt her lungs, between blasts.

At the next break, the next whisper of sweet, sweet promises of warmth, of relief, of freedom, if only she would repent her wicked ways, if only she would turn against everything that she was. Belle's bottom lip trembled, "Wait..." Her voice was hoarse from lack of use, lack of water to drink. One of the priests started toward her, and Belle shifted her head, slowly lifting it to look at him. But when she looked up, it wasn't the priest she looked at. It was the small red spot on the door in the distance... That wasn't normally there... That was different... The priest bent at the waist, his blank white mask blocking Belle's view of the one thing that didn't belong in the series of routines. "Wait..." She murmured again, leaning her body closer to the pillar to see around the priest. The priest continued his whisperings, offering her warmth, food, clothing, a hot bath, the world on a platter if she would just repent.

And then all hell broke loose.

A jet of fire burst through the door before it melted entirely. A large man stepped into the sterile room, a stark contrast with his bronze skin, dark hair, and swirling tattooed arms, his hand engulfed in fire. He was quickly followed by two others, a slender female and a tall man, and they were followed by a small group of five men in dark armor, in shades of red and black. The contrast had Belle laughing hollowly. Ice was white, ice was all she had seen, ice and the stormy eyes of the king, the father of her heart. And the rock... Was it now? Was this what King Davion had meant? Wasn't she supposed to do something to help? She would know when the time came; that's what he had alluded to. Even as if just thinking of the rock, it sparked to life, her chest started to warm, the rock radiating heat. With all the feeble strength she could muster, Belle sat up on her knees, bringing her shackled hands to the small pocket at her breast. She fished out the rock, holding it tightly in her hand while the exterior walls were covered in flame. Fucking comforting warmth. Belle could have cried at the first lick of the flame coming anywhere close to her. Warmth, she didn't care who the fuck this man was; she would let him burn her alive if it meant being warm.

She couldn't throw the stone, still bound to the pillar in the middle of the room as the walls wept, melting slowly after standing frozen for centuries. But she could kick it... Belle angled her wrists, dropping the stone on the ground in front of her before using the base of her foot to shove it toward the fire god, her savior. With a quick flick of a finger, he raised the stone from the ground and clapped it between his hands. Releasing a thunderous laugh as the crimson armored warriors made quick work of the remaining priests, cutting them down and setting their corpses alight, their stark white robes barely stained in red before the flames took them over.

The large, unfamiliar man rubbed his palms together before extending them. A black blade formed from the small

112

stone and sparked to life in his hand as he brandished a proud smile. Another man stood in the doorway. Belle knew it was King Davion before her eyes had fully locked onto him, with a small, handmade blade in his hand, bearing witness to the mayhem that had been unleashed.

The man who hadn't been dressed in red crouched next to Belle, her head rolling weakly in his direction. "I'm here." He muttered while cupping her face with one hand, the other releasing the shackles that held her to the pillar and held her magic at bay. "Can you walk?" He inquired while compelling her to look at him. The moment her hands were free, her body fell limply against him. Chaos broke out around them as a siren sounded, and the thundering sound of boots began to converge upon them from all directions.

Her brows stitched together, eyes cloudy from exhaustion and confusion from what she was seeing. Weakly, Belle reached up and cupped the man's familiar cheek before shifting her hand up to his scruffy hair. Had it been so long that Davion had grown his hair out? The stubble on his cheeks would at least partially corroborate her thought process. "Take what you need from me..." he whispered against her hair while he held her tight, his voice shook with something deeper than fear for her; it was desperation. "Please, Belle. Take it." For a breathless moment, she stayed still, hovering at the edge of herself, too weak, too lost, and too numb to move. Then the world came rushing into her, full color, full sense as that first tiny string of energy flowed from the man in front of her. Her lips brushed against the hollow of his throat, hesitant and trembling, and Donovan shuddered under her as his pulse skyrocketed. As the temporary binding thread was sewn through the needle that was their bodies, Donovan feathered a kiss just below her ear, and another at the delicate curve of her neck. A third at the hollow between her neck and shoulder. And another, lingering now at the top of her shoulder blade; he wanted her to remember, he begged her with his lips alone.

The feeling was so familiar that Belle withdrew from him even as her eyes shimmered gold, her hands braced on his shoulders as she continued to slowly, steadily, carefully pull energy from him. Her eyes were clear from the haze of the past two weeks now, and she froze, not from the cold, not from

113

fear, but from recognition. Her world tilted, and suddenly she wasn't dying on frozen stone anymore. She was back at the party that Khandra had taken her to, her hips being guided by an unseen man behind her, and the thought that she had even then that it couldn't have possibly been Donovan... But it had... It was Donovan. It had always been Donovan.

Before she could second guess herself, before guilt or fear or duty could claw its way in, Belle surged up, her hands framing his face as she kissed him. Hard. Desperate. Hungry. Not by accident, and not in a sense of confusion. Donovan made a soft, wrecked sound deep in his throat, giving her everything she asked for without hesitation.

Around them, the ice melted, and the world burned. Kaelith's controlled blaze reached the ceiling of the room now, intentionally ruining as much of this pristine hell as it could. "Daddy!" Khandra screamed, her voice breaking as she finally turned to King Davion and crashed into him, squeezing him with every bit of might she had.

The kiss between Donovan and Belle abruptly ended when Donovan heard not only Khandra screaming, but what she was screaming. He jolted to his feet, dark grey eyes scanning the room quickly. He saw Khandra clung to a man, much smaller than he had been years ago, much older, but the storm grey eyes he looked to Donovan with mirrored his own, and he knew.

"We are running out of time." Kaelith barked even as he sliced a guard down, the flame blade dancing through the air with his swift movement. "Get the Princess. We must leave." He ordered his men, and two of them turned on queue, aiming for Khandra. Donovan gave up on the idea of Belle walking out of this crystallized hell and picked her up, holding her tightly against his chest. "Your Highness." Kaelith tossed King Davion the flaming sword, formed from the heat stone he had given to Belle, and when he caught it, he was not burned by the flames but consumed by it. It melded to his arm, flames licking up his arm before almost ornately covering most of his body, a crown of fire circled at his head as Khandra was pried from him.

The King moved like he had been born for war. Each swing of the flame-lit sword cut down another guard, molten light carving through armor and flesh as the rebels surged past them. Kaelith and his warriors held the line ahead, driving the assault forward with steel and fire, but King Davion stayed at the rear, unbreakable, unyielding, the wall between his family and the men who had tortured him for years.

Khandra shoved her way back through the press of bodies until she reached her father, breath ragged, eyes wide as the tunnel exit came into view. They were almost free. Almost.

Then King Davion stopped. A high-pitched siren wail cried out all around them. The Holy Land was calling in reinforcements; they were funneling more guards straight through the very tunnels that they were using to escape. "Go," he ordered; low, calm, final.

Before any of them could protest, he lifted the sword overhead. Flame roared along the blade, reacting to Kaelith's magic like it recognized a brother, and the King brought it down in a brutal, sweeping arc. Fire met ice with a deafening crack. A sheet of frozen water peeled from the ceiling and slammed into place, sealing the entrance with a wall of jagged frost.

He stood on the other side of the ice alone, facing the legion of Holy Land soldiers who had waited years to reclaim him. And he didn't flinch.

Khandra screamed and ran for the sheet of ice, breaking free of the guards that tried to hold her. "No, no, no. Daddy!" Her hands had barely touched the ice before Kaelith's strong arm was wrapping around her middle, hauling her back. She went wild, flailing, kicking, and screaming, doing anything she could to try to get back to her father, to save him the way that he foolishly risked himself saving them all. Through the thick sheet of ice, King Davion placed his hand on it for just a moment, smiling at Khandra.

He wasn't afraid, he wasn't sad, he was proud. King Davion was imprisoned for Khandra. It was his bargaining chip to keep her free, to keep her safe. The witch of a Queen, once so full of life and joy, had told him that if she had a child with his 'useless' ability, she would have it killed or have him exiled. Why the two options were so dramatically paired was beyond King Davion; however, sure enough, their youngest, their only sweet baby girl showed signs of time manipulation from such a young age that he questioned if she would have any memory of him. Hearing her shriek for him damn near broke his heart; it spurred him on, drove him to fight the masses even harder, kill as many as he could before they would kill him, to save his family one last time.

The group staggered into the frozen night, steam still rising from their clothes, the snow hissing where Kaelith's fire magic brushed too close. Belle sagged in Donovan's arms, her head lolling against his shoulder. Her fingers twitched weakly against his chest, still clutching him, even unconscious, as if he might vanish if she let go. Even after feeding, she was still so very exhausted. Typically, when Belle pulled from Davion in training, there was a jolt, a shot of energy straight to her nerves. However, now, there was no energy burst, no adrenaline to put into her veins. Donovan barely breathed. He clutched her so tightly it hurt, as if trying to fuse her back together with sheer force.

He would be damned if he ever admitted it, but his body was sore. He would have let Belle drain him entirely in that awful room if it meant she would be okay, so he did everything in his power not to show just how much she had taken; just how close to collapsing he really wanted to be.

Kaelith had put Khandra back down once she agreed to stop fighting him, but in truth, she was so emotionally wrecked she could barely stand. She stumbled forward, her chest hollow and sore. She had just lost her father for the second time, and if she had just been faster... Kaelith grabbed her by the arms and pinned them to her sides. Her eyes snapped to him. "He chose this. He was a king, and chose to be a father to the last." He murmured low, only so the two of them could hear, "Honor him by living." He tucked a strand of her hair behind her ear. That was the final straw for her. She broke. Her knees buckled as the tears poured down her face, but Kaelith refused to let her hit the ground, scooping her into his arms, holding her against his warm chest.

Behind them, Kaelith's soldiers fanned out, setting wards, checking for pursuit. The wind howled across the barren tundra, empty and merciless. But the group stood; bruised, bloodied, and alive.

Alive.

Donovan dropped to one knee in the snow, still cradling Belle. He brushed a frozen lock of hair from her forehead with shaking fingers, his thumb ghosting over the faint shimmer of gold still clinging to her skin. "Belle..." He muttered, half because he just felt the need to say her name, as if it would solidify the reality that she was there in his arms. Belle stirred, the faintest motion.

Her lashes fluttered. For the first time in what felt like a lifetime, she looked up past Donovan, beyond the nightmare castle behind them, up into the endless night sky to the stars. Thousands of them, cold, bright, and real. Tears slid down Belle's face, freezing almost instantly. "You're free," Donovan whispered, even though she couldn't answer. "You're safe." Belle closed her eyes again, but this time, it wasn't from despair; it was trust, it was surrender, not to death, but to survival. And for the first time in two weeks, Belle let herself believe that maybe, just maybe, she would live.

Chapter 17

The next time Belle's eyes opened, she was in bed, surrounded by layers of heavy fabrics. She slowly inhaled, expecting the crystal-like sharpness of frozen air to penetrate her lungs, but when it didn't come, she slowly sat up, looking around. "You're awake." Khandra smiled from her chair not far from the bed, easing herself forward. "Men, in their typical fashion, felt that we females, in our delicate state, were in need of a proper rest before we continued on to Hightower." Khandra crossed the room and sat at the foot of the bed with Belle.

"Donovan!" Belle gasped and threw the blankets off herself before springing up from the bed. "You knew!" Belle threw her hands toward Khandra while her thoughts went wild, splintering in a hundred different directions, trying to put all the pieces together. "At the party. You had to have seen him. You had to have known." Khandra straightened her back and folded her hands into her lap.

"Couldn't start a revolution without a catalyst..." She kept her words metered, trained, calculated even, "There is still a lot you don't know, Belle. There is a lot that isn't in my place to explain. But Donovan needed to see you. He needed to know that you were okay." She shrugged her shoulders slightly, "I was just able to facilitate that in a way that wouldn't get anyone in any trouble... Except perhaps now, when he comes to see you and you likely throw something at his head." Her eyes shifted around the room, looking for anything that Belle could use as a weapon.

"Revolution?" Belle asked while looking around the small room, coming to a stop as she met a pair of dark grey eyes in the doorway. It took her breath away to see him standing there, arms folded over his chest, ankles crossed while leaning against the door frame. "What the actual fuck, Donovan?" Belle asked while crossing the room, shoving him hard in his chest. Donovan gave a little chuckle and stepped back on one foot to balance himself.

"Good to see you too, Belle." He wanted to wrap his arms around her and squeeze; he wanted to feel her body against his to know she was there, that outside of the torture she had just gone through, she was safe and healthy. But he knew her better than that; he knew if he tried right now, she would swing on him. "Yes, a revolution, Belle. An uprising my world has been in desperate need of for a long time. Khandra has been integral in organizing what she could from inside Hightower. Kaelith helped heal me and kept me safe and hidden from my brother and my mother. The pair of them... That is a complicated story entirely." Belle hardly noticed every step he took forward had her retreating to the point she fell back onto the bed.

"I'll leave you two to talk..." Khandra all but whispered while slipping out of the room, closing the door behind herself.

"What all has Davion told you?" Donovan asked while folding his arms over his chest, standing over Belle as she stared up at him. "The keys, the Holy Land, all of that... What has he told you?"

With a slow, steady breath, she began to unravel everything that had happened to her since she was literally pulled away from Donovan. "He first tried to convince me that you were the bad guy in this situation. That you stole the keys for your own purpose..." Belle scoffed and shook her head, trailing her fingernails at the edge of her lower lip. "Hell, Donovan, I haven't even had time to process you dying..." She angled toward him, "And you're not even dead." She added with another shrug. She reached her hands out to him even as he stood over her. "You're not dead." There was an ache in her chest, one that she couldn't fully make sense of, but Belle was beyond relieved that he wasn't dead.

It would take a lot more than a few arrows to kill me." He shrugged before shooing her slightly, motioning for Belle to

119

make room on the bed for him. They curled up together, his arm wrapped tightly around her as Belle lay her head on his chest, listening to the quiet, steady beat of his heart. "I am not the bad guy in this story... As much as Davion would have you believe otherwise." He began while gently running his fingers through her hair. "I took the keys and left when I found out that the Queen was working with The Holy Land. They want to control all the realms. They want to subjugate everyone to their beliefs and their practices only. With the knowledge that your world has no magic in it, they would seem like gods." Donovan rolled his eyes. "So... to prevent it. I took the keys and ran to the only place I thought was going to be safe."

He told her about the weeks he spent hiding in the shadows, finding the best way to blend into Belle's world. Donovan spoke about an unknown force that pulled him to the orphanage that Belle was at; and ever since then, there had been what felt like an invisible tether pulling him back to her. "Surprise... I'm a succubus." She interjected, bringing them both to chuckle.

"The key... The one that brought us both here, that I took from you in that field... It found its way to Khandra." He blinked a few times, thinking back to Belle so utterly confused in the field, and Donovan desperately willing that key to safety through his shadows. "It appeared to her. She appeared to me. We appeared to Kaelith. They've got some of the best healers in Obsera, entire libraries dedicated to books on healing, old ways and new. He kept me safe, kept my existence quiet. Until I was healthy enough to come for the key." He leaned down and placed a little kiss on the top of Belle's head.

"That's why you were at the party?" Belle asked quietly, her eyes drifting closed. "Perfect distraction to steal something from the castle... Lure the guard... Davion... away so that you can get in and out undetected..." She pursed her lips and nodded a little. "I taught you well." Belle laughed.

"You did... and to always have a man... or in this case, woman on the inside..." He cut himself off when Belle jolted up, honey brown eyes wide with panic. "What? What is it?"

"Ivory." Belle pushed herself out of bed, bare feet padding around the room. "The Holy Land has another way to get to other realms." She hadn't even begun to explain and was

120

already breathless, thinking back to the conversation between herself and Ivory. "My inside person... It was always Ivory." She was speaking slowly, with the intention of not tripping over her words. "Ivory is here. White cloak, magic... all of it. Ivory works for them. They were so insistent on me stealing that damn key because they needed it back for their..." She waved her hands around, not able to find the words, "They didn't know that I am... whatever the fuck I am. Feed... Feed..." She wrinkled her face up before pinching the bridge of her nose. "Ivory said something about the power was always there... It just needed to be fed."

Donovan watched her like she was a tiny tornado swirling around the room. He tilted his head and folded his arms over his chest while he followed her with his eyes. Of course, The Holy Land found another way to travel between realms... He had ruined that for them when he took the keys... So they made another way... Fuckers. "Fed?" He echoed, thinking back to how unusually empty the cages all seemed in comparison to what everyone had expected to find.

Belle shrugged her shoulders up high before dropping them defeated, her eyes narrowed, still thinking it through. "Your guess is better than mine, I'm sure." Folding her arms over her chest, she dropped back onto the bed, "The only time I was outside of my cage was to be tortured..." Her breath hitched, catching in her throat when her mind took her back to the constant flow of frozen water that assaulted her for what felt like hours on end.

"We can try to make more sense of it when we get back." Donovan nodded while leaning toward Belle, stroking her arm reassuringly. "Sit back here. Let me try to fill some of the gaps." It wasn't necessarily an order, but Donovan patted the bed next to himself, and Belle lazily climbed back up next to him once more. "Try not to jump up so fast next time, your big head nearly knocked me out..." He jabbed, joking with her.

"Next time I'll just knock you out. Your brother has had me training for weeks. I'm a lean, mean, ass kicking machine at this point." Belle scoffed and shook her head as she adjusted, leaning her head against his chest once more. The jest shared between the two of them felt natural, normal, and somewhere, a weight felt like it lifted from her core, her very soul just having a shred of normalcy back in her world.

Donovan watched her quietly, allowing her to settle back against him before he wrapped an arm around her body, holding her in place against him, where he felt she always deserved to be. "According to Khandra... my dear brother has had you doing a lot of things..." He huffed out a breath and pulled his hands through his hair. Belle winced at the words, despite there being no intended sting in them. Donovan looked down at Belle when he felt her tense. "We were never exclusive, Belle..." He assured her through his own brand of pain while trying to tell Belle that it was okay that she had slept with his brother. "Besides, I'm chalking it up to him looking too much like me and I'm just irresistible..." He added with a little shrug, smiling faintly when Belle's shoulders shook from quiet laughter. "Anyway... Khandra says her spies have noticed he hasn't been the same since you were taken..." Belle pouted her lips slightly, "I think your impact on him, and what our mother has done to you, may be one of the most eye-opening things for him. Though he still will not be welcoming me back with open arms for sure."

Chapter 18

They talked for a long time, so long that Belle, still not fully healed, had to rest. Donovan had curled up in the small bed with her, she stayed with her head on his chest, feeling his fingertips through her hair. She fell into the first real sleep she had had in weeks. Not the desperate sleep that came at the end of a long day of training with Davion. Not the sleep that finally overtook her as Belle had wondered if it was the last time that she would fall asleep in that frozen hellscape altogether. A genuinely relaxed sleep. Donovan did his best to keep the subject matter light when he felt her body start to relax against his. He told her about Kaelith's castle, the constant summer heat, the towering obsidian spikes of the castle, and the desert style gardens that Kaelith, the giant fireball of a man, loved to walk daily.

The passing thought of never returning to her world had crossed her mind, but what did she really have left for herself back in New York? A decent paying job that, if it ever went sideways, would end with her in jail for the rest of her life, a few people in her life that she very loosely called friends, more like acquaintances than anything. That number dwindled one less even here with Ivory's deep-rooted betrayal. Here, in Donovan and Davion's world, she had power, and she was slowly finding her purpose when sleep finally took her; her final waking thought being that The Holy Land had other ways to travel the realms.

The harsh light of morning woke her as it peered through the window, beaming directly on her face. Belle sprang up, grimacing at the aches and pains as her body protested such a sudden movement as she looked around. Donovan stirred from under her, slowly inhaling as he opened his eyes. "Well, well, well..." He began with a slight smirk. "It has been a very long time since we woke up in the same bed." He offered with a lopsided grin.

Though Belle rolled her eyes at him, she fell back down onto his chest, draping an arm over his body, "I have always had such a love-hate relationship with your bullshit, Donovan." She nodded as he slid his arms around her, holding her tightly. The cocky attitude hid his insecurities; it always had. Now, Donovan feared that when they returned to the castle, Belle would fall back into Davion's arms instead of his. They weren't exactly the perfect couple, or even a couple at all, when they fell into this mess. He did his best to hide his frustration as she lay on his chest. He was still mad at himself that she fell into this in the first place, even if she did technically belong. The human world, Belle's world, had no magic, not anymore anyway; it had all been squashed, burned, forgotten, or just generally stomped out. There were glimpses here and there of it, but it was instantly demonized, of course. Donovan had no idea of the power Belle held; even if it was only part of her genetics, part human, part fae; maybe that was how she ended up in the orphanage in the first place... "When do we head back to the castle?" She asked quietly, still sleepy, snapping Donovan out of his thoughts.

"We start that way today. With both the Holy Land and surely Hightower on alert, we can't risk using a portal." He said quietly, through a tinge of something he silently labeled as jealousy... Was Belle in a hurry to get back to Davion? Was she so anxious to get rid of him and fall back into his brother's bed? Through a huffed breath, he gave her side a gentle squeeze, "Let's get dressed, I'm sure Kaelith is ready to get back to the warmth of Obsera." He buried his worry, knowing that there were more important things than the worry of who this beautiful woman could choose to be with in the end.

Of course, Donovan had been right. Khandra was bundled from head to toe in furs for warmth and still stood close to Kaelith. Kaelith radiated warmth, even in the snow-covered terrain of the Holy Land, as if he were a flame incarnate. His broad, bare arms were folded over his chest as he stood in front of Khandra, chatting quietly while Donovan and Belle approached. "You stay close to me until we get out of here. The last thing we need is you freezing to death." Kaelith's voice was deep, and there was an edge to it that hadn't been there yesterday; the cold was wearing on him.

Belle shrugged and stepped between Khandra and Kaelith, instantly grateful for the heat that fell from the large man. Forever the playful fae, Khandra opened her thick fur jacket and wrapped herself around Belle. "Gods alive, we would never hear the end of it from either of the boys if something happened to her now." Khandra rested her chin on Belle's shoulder, having to hunch down just slightly due to their height difference.

Without the use of portals at their disposal, they were relegated to much slower forms of travel. To leave Holy Land territory, they purchased passage on a small ship, Donovan, the most unrecognizable of the group doing the talking for everyone.

Crossing back into Hightower territory was a welcome reprieve after the longest journey had worn itself into already aching bones. Leaving the Holy Land meant crossing the vast stretch of sea that divided their territories, a league of water that nearly swallowed the horizon whole. For once, fortune favored them; the sea lay still and silver, and no shadows stirred beneath the waves.

No one dared speak of it aloud, but every soul aboard was silently grateful they had not drawn the attention of the Drowned Court and their draconic leviathan. Among sailors, it was said that to name the Court at sea was to summon them, and when the leviathan rose, it did not leave witnesses. The unlucky were dragged beneath the surface, their lungs filled with brine until they joined the endless procession of the drowned.

Belle sat quietly, staring around at sailors and Donovan as they all moved cautiously across the deck of the ship, each step carefully taken as if a false move could send a ripple that would summon their end. "What..." Belle started to ask Khandra, but she shook her head and put a finger to her lips, silencing the questioning.

"Different world... Different dangers..." Donovan whispered to Belle, narrowing his eyes slightly as he talked, choosing his words carefully. "Respecting the waters is the smartest choice." He nodded now, pleased with himself for not dooming them all to a dark, wet, grave.

They all knew when they crossed back into Hightower territory. It was like stepping through a doorway from one season to another. The air warmed instantly, even as they still crossed the sea. When they finally docked and were brought to land, the grass went from being hard, dead, and covered in snow to soft, lush, and green. The air that was so cold it pricked at their lungs shifted to the perfect temperature, a beautiful spring day in Belle's mind. Until she remembered the hell that waited for her back at the castle.

Kaelith and his small band of warriors made their exit, earning a lofted brow and curious look from Belle to Khandra when the King of the Wildelands bowed and kissed Khandra's hand before taking his leave. Khandra gave Belle the faintest shrug and raised her brows with a knowing smile before shifting to link her arms with Belle.

The remainder of the journey for the day was spent with a lot of chatting between the three of them. The conversation ranged from talking about Belle's world and how she grew up with Donovan, to what she did in her world, to talk of the rebellion, the plans, the goals; and the strongest of which stuck in Belle's mind was de-throning the Queen... Belle had a bone to pick with her... or break on her... It likely depended on the Queen herself.

They walked straight into the castle, none of the guards flinched at seeing Belle or Khandra, but the whispers began as soon as they realized who the scruffy man who accompanied them was. A small redheaded servant, with eerie green eyes that nearly gave off a light of their own, gasped sharply before turning on her heel, rushing away quickly. Surely Davion would know before they got to him; surely, he would be on the prowl or the attack by the time they made it to the throne room.

Belle pushed the large, heavy double doors open, allowing them to swing wide as the trio stepped into the throne room. Someone had moved a long oval-shaped table into the center of the room, a table designed for war... Davion sat at the head, surrounded by high mages and other ranking officials of the court. The room went silent; all eyes shifted to the trio as they approached the table. "Out. Now." Belle barked, her eyes glued to Davion. All of her confidence shook under the weight of their eyes locked to one another. Belle knew that she didn't have any power in this room; she knew that she was a nobody to the people that sat in their fancy robes and their glittering jewelry, but the hell if she was going to let that stop her now.

Chapter 19

Her sentiment was echoed by Davion with just as much authority as Belle used. "Out." One word had them all scattering, heavy wooden chairs scraped across the stone floor as they pushed from the table before hurrying out. "Close the damned door." He called after the little crowd that all but ran for the door. His eyes never left Belle; he scanned her from top to bottom, assessing her tangled hair, her hollowed eyes, her cracked lips, the scraps of fabric that she wore, and the way that her shoulders began to sag despite herself.

Before Belle could start in on Davion, before she could fully form a sentence to start cursing him for the lies, the betrayal, and everything that came with it, Davion was on her, his hands cupped ever so gently at her cheeks. "Belle..." Her name fell from his lips like a breathless prayer. His thumb smoothed gently over her cheek. Still keeping her face in his hands, he took a small step back, looking her over once more now that he stood closer. She still wore the tattered rag of a dress the Holy Land had put her in, all but useless slippers that were about to fall apart on her feet. Her hair was still tangled, knotted from neglect. She stared up at him, her feelings guarded, protected like it was behind a wall of ice; ice she had been trapped in for what felt like forever. Davion wasn't so easy to hide his feelings; they ranged from anger to excitement to pure, blind rage.

His gaze finally shifted from Belle as his hands slid down her face, trailing the sides of her neck, down her shoulders, and coming to rest at her upper arms. He looked at his sister, first giving her a small nod of gratitude. Then Davion's eyes fell to

Donovan. Donovan tilted his head up slightly, jutting his chin out while straightening his stance. Davion took a step towards Donovan, and Belle grabbed his wrist, bare flesh in her grip. Davion's eyes went wide as he looked back at Belle. She was pulling from him, she was doing it so controlled, as if it was natural to her, and Davion knew that feeling... He knew that the pull that made him feel like something was being yanked from his core was just a warning, just a taste of the power that Belle could pull if she felt the need to. "Why would you attack the person who brought me back? You're not stupid, Davion."

He cocked his head slightly while watching Belle drop his hand; the coolness at his flesh that replaced her hand left him wanting more, craving her touch, her pull, and the pleasure and delight it brought with it. From his peripheral vision, he saw Donovan take a step toward Belle, as if Davion was the threat here, as if he was going to be the one to hurt her. He would like to say he truly heard what Belle had said, but his eyes locked onto his brother's again, and truthfully, he hadn't been listening. Not really. The rage festered up again, territorial and possessive, clawing to the surface.

Belle knew there was no time to argue, nor did she really have the energy to try to hold either of them back while they had a silent territorial pissing match. She just wanted to tell them to whip out their dicks and get the contest over with, but they were twins... logically... they'd be the same. Without warning, she spun on Davion, reaching up and grabbing his jaw in one sharp motion, nails pressing roughly into his cheeks. His jaw slacked just enough for Belle to spit into his mouth. She heard Khandra gasp, surely clutching her metaphorical pearls, but there were more important matters at hand; "Calm the fuck down." Her words were sharp, punctuated, and deliberate; moreover, her words were layered with her magic, pouring straight through Davion.

His body locked in place, a faint shudder rolling down his spine as her succubus influence took hold. Though his muscles still begged him to move, and his mind roared with fury, he couldn't move. His heaving chest settled into deep, slow breaths as he was pulled deep under Belle's control, and somewhere under the haze and internal battle of emotions and

129

ability was a thought that Davion only let himself see as semi-welcomed. *Why the hell was that so godsdamned hot...*

The haze in his mind settling into a forced calm, Davion took a slow breath to speak through gritted teeth, his jaw still half-caught under Belle's palm. "Clever," he rasped, faintly shaking his head. "Rude... but clever."

Belle smirked, patting his cheek twice before smirking, stepping back. "You're welcome."

A beat of heavy silence stretched between the four of them, the air still thick with unspoken tension. It was Khandra who moved first, her voice cool and deliberate. "Enough. We should sit." She gestured toward the table. "This conversation needs clarity, not posturing."

Without waiting for an argument, Khandra stepped toward one of the empty seats and claimed it, lowering herself gracefully. Belle followed, exhaustion pulling at her limbs, though she held her head high as she dropped into the chair beside Khandra unceremoniously. Even the energy she had pulled from Davion couldn't touch the level of exhaustion that lingered over every inch of her body.

Davion drew in a long breath through his nose, forcing the last edges of fury down. He stalked toward the head of the table and seated himself, movements sharp but controlled. The quieter, more logical side of his brain knew at this point, they were all on the same side, and there was no more reason to attack Donovan. But he had been with Belle in the past; who is to say it hadn't happened again during their escape from The Holy Land? He let out an uncomfortable grunt as he lowered himself into his chair, knuckles turning white on the arms of it; all the discourse in his mind surrounding the 'what if' thoughts growing louder and louder.

Donovan, of course, was the only one who seemed utterly unbothered. He strolled up, plucked one of the half-finished glasses of wine abandoned on the table, and tipped it lazily toward his brother in mock salute before taking a slow sip as he lowered himself in a chair opposite Khandra and Belle.

"Donovan," Davion growled, his eyes narrowing, issuing a small warning.

"What?" Donovan's mouth twitched into a smirk. "After all that, you looked like you needed it more than I did. I was

130

just too thirsty to share. Besides... you've got your own cup. We don't need to share."

Before Davion could snap back, Khandra chimed in, her tone cutting clean through the room. "We don't have time for one of your pissing matches. There are bigger problems at hand."

Belle nodded slightly before propping her chin in her hand, pinning Davion with her eyes as just the corners of her lips tipped up into an intentional smile. "Start talking." As Davion straightened, she held up a finger, "Let's be specific here... Start talking about what has happened since I was thrown into that frozen hellscape..." She couldn't keep her smile from growing when Davion's eye twitched at the command laced with succubus magic.

Davion's fingers flexed against the polished surface of the table as he felt the compulsion of her words ripple through him. He held her stare a beat longer, then exhaled slowly. "Belle..." His voice softened. "I didn't know. I had no idea my mother would have stooped so low. I was unaware how tangled she was with the Holy Land... how deep her ties ran inside their walls." Donovan scoffed, rolling his eyes in a silent '*told you so*' fashion on display for everyone to see.

It was Belle who straightened now, her gaze flicking down to the half-eaten plate of food before her. The ice behind her eyes thawed, but only barely.

"She was called to the Holy City, according to Courtland," Davion continued. "I didn't know what for. She wouldn't tell me. Now I know. It was because of *you*." He gestured loosely toward the trio in front of him. "When I asked Khandra for help... I knew it had to have been Donovan."

He paused, shaking his head, not at Donovan's name, but at how blind he'd been. How many things had he gotten wrong because of their mother? The way he'd treated Donovan. How close he'd come to killing him. A conversation for another time.

"Yes, yes, I helped save Donovan," Khandra said, voice smooth. "I helped keep him hidden. Kept feeding him information while he recovered in the Wildelands, thanks to your guards' pitiful attempt at murdering royalty. Shame, shame... Bad Khandra. How dare I keep such big secrets?"

131

Khandra rolled her wrist, hurrying the conversation along partly to avoid the awkwardness of it, but more so for Belle, that poor woman needed to rest, and more healing than Khandra knew she could provide.

The three of them blinked at Khandra, and then collectively, slowly nodded. "With Kaelith's help, I've started building a rebellion. The numbers don't come anywhere close to Hightower soldiers, but they're strong. I have the support of Kaelith's Razshan as well." He nodded toward Belle, "His elite soldiers; some of them were with us when we rescued you. They're... brutal... to say the very least..." Donovan gave a little shrug. "Knowing what we've known on our side, mother and her ties, well... suspected ties... We were building to take on Hightower and The Holy Land. But now..."

Khandra interjected before Donovan could say something to antagonize Davion all over again, "We are hoping because you know the truth now, Davion, the troops here will rally behind you, and we would have enough able-bodied fighters to rival those of The Holy Land. Not to mention, in a battle of ice versus fire, fire would likely win."

"They have another way to cross the realms." Belle blurted, albeit exhaustion covering any other emotion that she could've carried. "I had an associate back in my world, they were..." Belle narrowed her eyes and shook her head, searching for the proper words. With a huff of an exhale, she continued, "They were there, they told me that The Holy Land had another way of crossing the realms, but that it just needed to be fed." Khandra tensed next to Belle, and Davion sat up straight, face unreadable.

"What does that mean?" Khandra asked, looking between her brothers. When neither of them made a move to start answering, she continued, "What does it need to be fed? There's no need for a key now if they have other ways of traveling..."

"It also means that they are now closer to their goal of dominating all realms." Donovan scrubbed his hands through his hair before sitting back in the chair, doing his best not to shoot a glare at his brother for never having listened to him in the first place.

132

Belle had shifted in her seat, resting back against it, elbow braced on one of the arms of the chair, head in her palm, body relaxing. As all eyes moved back to Davion, knowing this moment hinged on him and his word to bring the Hightower soldiers, Khandra reached for Belle, gently placing her hand on Belle's arm. Belle shivered, the little hairs on her arm standing at attention as Khandra's magic worked its way through her body, the cooling sensation traveling from the point of contact as Khandra pulled back the time on the wounds and ache of Belle's body. Silently, Khandra's gaze shifted from Davion to Belle as she felt her magic hit a wall within Belle; her fingers curled around Belle's arm as if more solid contact could break the wall down. Belle bit her lower lip as she turned to Khandra, shaking her head slightly; some damage couldn't be undone, not even with time on their side, and at that moment, Belle knew it had been final. "I would like to rest." She announced suddenly, a ball of emotion forming in her throat. "Khandra can take me while you two figure out the strategy. I assume that Sadie will be happy I'm back."

Khandra got the hint and took the lead. "Yes, let's leave the boys to plan a war. You need rest, and I need a bath." She carried a light, nonchalant air to her tone despite the wave of confusion she was hiding from them. Both men nodded, and the women departed.

Once safely in the hall, Khandra locked her arm around Belle's, standing close. "What was that?" She asked and gripped Belle tighter when Khandra felt her tense.

Khandra's arm tightened around her as they moved through the quiet hall. The moment they were out of earshot, Khandra spoke again, voice softer but edged with concern. "What's wrong?" she asked, fingers flexing slightly where they gripped Belle's arm. "You tensed... I felt it."

Belle swallowed hard, her throat thick. The weight of exhaustion pressed down on her shoulders, on her chest, but it wasn't the physical strain that finally cracked her walls. It was the knowledge she'd carried alone. The part she hadn't dared to speak aloud. Somehow Belle knew that Khandra's magic had worked its way to the wound she had hoped wasn't real in the first place, and that was her tipping point... She slowed, steps faltering, and Khandra stopped with her. Belle's voice came low—barely above a whisper. "There's something you should know." Khandra waited, as patiently as she could manage.

Belle's eyes burned. Her gaze dropped to the floor. "In the prison... the moment you cross through the threshold of that hell... the women there..." Her breath hitched. "They... they sterilize them. All of them." Instinctively, she pulled her arms away from Khandra and wrapped them low around her stomach.

Khandra's breath caught, sharp and audible as she pulled back from Belle. Not in disgust of her, but disgust for taking something so sacred, and her mother having been the root of it.

Belle pressed on, words tumbling before she could lose her nerve. "It wasn't a choice. They didn't tell me until it was done. It was... part of the processing. Routine, they said." She swallowed hard, drawing a ragged breath, her voice cracked. "I can't... I can't have children. Not anymore." Khandra's heart twisted as the first sob fell free from Belle's lips. Khandra wrapped her arms around Belle, squeezing her tightly even as they both collapsed to the floor. "I never gave children a thought, but at least I had the option... and now..." words failed her as the tears took over.

"Oh, Belle..." she whispered. "I'm so sorry." Khandra held her tight, rubbing her back. She understood the wall her magic ran into now, a jagged, pointed, vicious wall that all but clawed back as her gentle magic tried to heal Belle. "Selune..." Khandra whispered, and a small female Elf appeared at their side. "Find Sadie... tell her Belle has returned and will need a bath first. We will be along shortly." Selune nodded and vanished.

Belle curled against Khandra as they both sat tangled together on the floor and started to shake. Khandra looked down, puzzled as she heard Belle start to... laugh... Khandra's head tilted to the side. "When do I get a little elf spy?" Belle asked while looking up to Khandra, wiping her eyes.

Khandra breathed out a light laugh, "Not until you have Hightower magic." She eased back from Belle, standing from the floor, "Come on, lovely, let's get you cleaned up." Belle nodded and took Khandra's outstretched hand.

Chapter 20

Khandra left Belle at the doorway to her quarters, and once inside, the door safely closed behind her, Belle sighed heavily, closing her eyes while shuffling her feet forward. "Belle!" She was almost bulldozed by Sadie, wrapping her arms around Belle so tightly that she thought her ribs might pop. "Selune told me you were back, but I thought it was a lie... No one comes back from The Holy Land... Well... those that aren't guests anyway..." She scoffed and waved a dismissive hand as she stepped back, taking a moment to truly look at Belle; there was a flash of sadness in her eyes that Sadie quickly pushed away, knowing Belle wouldn't be looking for sympathy. "Let's get you into the bath. We have so much to catch up on." She masked her pain with her typical joyful voice as she guided Belle into the bathing chambers.

Belle was quickly running out of what little energy she had left. She was thankful to be able to slump her shoulders, to not stand on ceremony, to not have to hold the weight of everything on her shoulders, even if only for a short while. Allowing Sadie to guide her, knowing the woman would soon wash her naked body, was a far cry from where she had been when she first landed in this strange place. So many things had changed in what felt like only days. "How long have I been here?" Belle questioned while allowing Sadie to peel off what was left of the rags she had been brought back in.

Sadie made a little humming sound while she dropped the tattered fabric on the floor, "I believe a little longer than two fortnights... A month, perhaps." Her tone sang of uncertainty in her own words. "So many things have shifted in the time you've been..." Her words died off, seeing all the bruises on Belle's body as she held her hand out to help Belle into the bath. Belle's body practically melted into the water, and a sob broke free from her before she could stop it.

"Please tell me." As much as Belle would've loved the silence, she didn't think being alone with her own thoughts was wise, and hearing Sadie tell her about what had happened in Hightower since her absence would keep her mind from spiraling.

Sadie took a deep breath before biting down on her lip, her brow wrinkling as she began to wash Belle's body. "Something changed in the prince." She began while lifting Belle's limp arm. "He no longer blindly obeys his mother. He has been..." She tilted her head to the side slightly, "Empty? Since you've been gone. He is rarely seen outside of his quarters unless necessary. He often makes quips of open defiance against the Queen, and the longer you've been gone, the more brazen he seems to be growing... As if your absence has truly opened his eyes." She continued to scrub layers and layers of filth and dirt from Belle, being as gentle and thorough as possible before pausing to lean in toward Belle, adding quietly, "Davion has been plotting something, planning an uprising against the queen... Low staff are not supposed to know, but we have our ways..." Belle straightened slightly, angling to look at Sadie.

"Uprising?" She questioned, "What do you mean uprising?" Sadie gave a little shrug, pursing her lips.

"No one knows. Or if they do know, they have found the strength and loyalty to not bend or break their word." Belle huffed out a slight chuckle, her jaw slacking while she tilted her head back so Sadie could begin working on her hair.

Despite the delicious gossip, Belle found herself more conflicted. Having talked to Donovan on the journey back to Hightower, she had begun to force her heart away from Davion, seeing him for the villain he had always been, but now, she wasn't too sure. "Where is Maude?" Belle asked absently as she closed her eyes while Sadie began to untangle the mess.

"Dismissed. Davion questioned her loyalty and felt it would be better that, upon your return, you had someone you trusted with you." She was talking about herself, and it made Belle smile to think Davion hadn't given up on Belle coming back to

Hightower. "He has been working his way through the staff, the guards, the army; all of us, and anyone blindly following the Queen simply because she is the one with the crown, or those he feels would report back to her directly, have all been dismissed. He sat down with me, apologized for his years of attitude, and asked about my loyalty to you directly." Sadie gave a little shrug, as if there was ever a question about Sadie being loyal. "I want to see you wear the crown." She admitted before biting down on her lower lip once more. "I think your outside perspective to our realm would benefit the people. You were the first person in a very long time to stand up to Davion, to challenge him and make him be polite." She laughed now, "If that is who you truly are at heart, the people of Hightower would be so lucky to have you as their queen."

Belle sat up once more, slowly turning toward Sadie, "That would require the Queen being dead, and for Davion..." She trailed off, wrinkling her brow, "Or Donovan to take the throne..." Belle scrunched up her face and groaned before allowing herself to slide entirely under the water, letting bubbles trail up. What would she do if it came down to choosing one of them? What would she do if it meant breaking one of their hearts? Sadie wiggled her fingers in the water, and Belle came back up for air. "I don't want to have to choose..." Belle wrinkled her nose now while Sadie dutifully went back to her hair.

"So don't." She said it so plainly, so simply, Belle couldn't help but laugh. "Choose both. Choose neither. You take the crown; you keep the crown."

"You know... Where I'm from... in any story involving any kind of fae, they always speak in riddles, and the people dealing with them always get annoyed..." Belle extended a finger toward Sadie while nodding, "I'm really starting to understand now." Belle smiled and shook her head before letting it rest back, allowing Sadie to work through two weeks' worth of knots and tangles and gods only knew what else ended up in there.

By the time that Belle was deemed clean enough to leave the tub, Sadie had drained and refilled the tub once, the water being too dirty to continue, and, honestly, Belle was thankful for it. Some people deep clean their houses... Sadie deep cleaned Belle. "I will fetch you some food," Sadie said with a hopeful grin before all but bouncing out of Belle's quarters.

Belle held the robe closed while lowering herself to the vanity chair, brushing out the few remaining tangles in her hair, looking at herself in the mirror for the first time in what felt like forever. Her cheeks were a little hollower, the bags under her eyes were awful, and her lips were dry and chapped. Even her collarbones seemed to stick out a bit further than they had. "Two weeks of starvation and I look like a wraith..." She muttered to herself before putting the brush down and quietly crossing the room to the couch nearest the fire. Kaelith's warmth had been nice, considering he was a walking, talking, fireball; but now, sitting by the fire on plush cushions, in clothing that was more than just a rag...

The heaviest sigh escaped her lips as she lay her head against the back of the couch, her eyes drifting closed. For just a minute in the silence of her room, she was able to reflect on absolutely everything that had happened in the month she had been in this realm. From literally falling into this strange storybook world, to thinking one of her oldest and most dearest friends was murdered. Then falling in love with... She sat up straight, eyes wide. "The fuck?" She muttered to herself, heart pounding in her chest. Had she fallen in love with Davion? She wrinkled her brow and looked around the room as if the answer was going to be there in a neon blinking sign. She had always loved Donovan; she grew up in love with the boyish charm and the goofy smile that he got when he was intentionally trying to make her laugh. Sadie's words echoed in her head, *"Choose both. Choose neither."*

As if summoned by her thoughts alone, the door to her chamber creaked open, the space outside enveloped by both men. "Jesus Christ..." She muttered to herself with a sigh. "Come in."

Both men stepped forward at the same time, and both men recoiled together, their shoulders thumping together between each other and the door frame. "Ugh. No. Please. After you, your royal highness." Donovan took a step back dramatically, using his arms to usher Davion into the room first while rolling his eyes.

138

Davion shot his brother a tight glare before finally stepping inside. "You're impossible."

Donovan followed with a grin that didn't quite reach his eyes. "And yet, here you are. Following my lead again."

Belle groaned, dragging a throw pillow over her face for a second before chucking it in the general direction of them. "I was promised recovery time, not time watching two magical testosterone goblins posture like stags in a rut. Sit. Both of you. If you're going to haunt my chamber like underworld ghouls, you can at least do it politely. Or I'll tell Khandra you're both being twats." They froze at that, just for a moment, as if the threat of Khandra was penultimate to death, then both silently moved to opposite ends of the sitting area like overgrown schoolboys sent to opposite corners. Belle stared at them for a long beat, her robe cinched tight, her legs tucked beneath her on the cushions. "So. Are you going to talk to me like functioning adults, or do I have to throw something heavier next time?"

Davion exhaled slowly, sitting with his back straight against the chair, hands resting on the arms, fingers absently drumming at the edge. "We didn't come to fight."

Donovan glanced sideways at him. "That's... new." He shoved his shaggy hair out of his face and did his best not to roll his eyes.

"Stop," Belle said softly. The fire cracked, warm and low beside her. "I know things are broken, especially between the two of you. And even more so between the three of us... But I'm tired. And I'm hurt. And I really, really need both of you to stop pretending like I don't matter in this." Both men looked at her now, really looked, seeing just how worn down and tired she was, despite handling it so well. She continued, her voice a little rough. "Donovan... I thought you were dead... I..." She swallowed hard, "I had no choice in you being left in the field... Davion... you locked me away, and you lied to me. You've both lied to me. You've both done shit that makes my chest hurt when I think about it. But I also know that I never stopped loving you. Either of you."

Donovan stood first. Slowly. Walking toward her like she might vanish. "I thought I was protecting you," he said. "I was wrong." He knelt in front of Belle, gently taking her hand into his.

Davion's jaw flexed. "I... never knew how to protect you without controlling everything. If I wasn't the one in charge, I was afraid I would lose you..." There was an undeniable hurt in his voice, "And I thought I did..."

Belle tilted her head back against the cushion, closing her eyes for a second. "Then maybe it's time you both try doing it *my* way."

Donovan remained on his knees in front of her, his hands resting on her thigh as he looked up at her. Davion stood from his chair and crossed to them both, sitting next to Belle, wrapping an arm around her as if to pull her closer, but also to not take her away from Donovan. "We have all been wrong in this little circle here, and there is nothing we can do to go back; only forward." Davion, suddenly the voice of reason, nodded while looking at his brother, a silent apology, a silent acceptance; after a moment, Donovan nodded as well.

The silence stretched again, this time heavy with *something else*. Belle opened her eyes and looked between them. "We can talk more later. Fight more later. Apologize and fall apart and whatever else we're supposed to do. But right now..." She reached for one of Donovan's hands. Then one of Davion's. Her thumb brushed both of their knuckles. "...right now, I need to feel alive again."

Davion's thumb stroked gently at Belle's shoulder, easing the fabric of the robe down as he looked at his brother. His free hand moved the fabric of the robe from Belle's thigh, pulling it back to expose her to Donovan. "Make her feel alive, Donovan..." It wasn't necessarily a command, but Donovan needed no more invitation from anyone. He shifted his grasp on Belle's hand, his stormy eyes shifting to look up to Belle for acceptance. She responded by spreading her legs for him.

He wasted no time, feathering kisses from her knee, up her inner thigh, to her pelvis, and finally spreading her with his tongue, one languid lick before he sealed his lips over her core, his tongue twirling devilishly around her clit.

Belle's breath hitched instantly, and her head fell back against Davion's arm; as a moan threatened to escape her lips, Davion claimed it, crushing his lips to hers. The hand that had

140

started it all trailed from her hip, up her stomach, between her breasts, and his fingers wrapped around her throat, smiting the next whisper of a moan as he looked down at Belle as her eyes went hazy with lust. He licked his lips, tasting hers on his, and knew the three of them were doomed.

Donovan and Belle seemed to have the same realization at the same time when their eyes locked as he licked his lips. He slid a finger into her, and she arched her back, letting out a soft moan that sent a pulse of magic through the air, heightening all their senses. Donovan pulled back and blinked once while looking at Belle; he felt the pull of her magic, and he knew the mountain he was about to dive off.

"Take me to bed." Belle all but purred the words, and in one fluid motion, Donovan stood, picking Belle up and carrying her to the bed, Davion already in tow. Feeling her body touch the bed, Belle shimmied out of the robe, leaving it discarded as she crawled up the mattress, beckoning both men to join her. She sat, propped on her arms, her legs spread wide.

Donovan crawled up after her, taking his place between her legs once more. Belle's head fell back as he resumed drinking her in, his tongue gliding through her, his saliva mixing with her slickness.

Davion loosened his pants as he knelt on the bed in front of Belle; removing his length from their constraints, he lofted his brows while smirking at her. "Open up." Two words, but the tone of command was all she needed to obey. Belle licked at her lips before opening her mouth wide as she tilted her head up to look at him.

Davion never knew how to be gentle, how not to be selfish and take for himself, and if truth be told, his restraint was the thinnest string being pulled tighter and bound to snap. Tentatively, he reached his hand out, cupping the back of her head as he slid his length deep into her mouth; the slowness of it sending a shiver up his spine. It was timed perfectly with Donovan sliding his finger back into Belle's center. She groaned against the length of Davion and let her eyes roll back.

Here in this moment, Belle felt no pain; the tiredness that pierced her to her core had been replaced by so much more. Davion tensed his jaw, hissing out a breath as he withdrew from Belle before thrusting forward into her mouth. The moan that bubbled in Belle's throat sent forth another wave of pleasure over the three of them.

Donovan nipped at Belle, and her hands flew to Davion's thighs, nails biting into his flesh while he held his length buried deep in Belle's throat, preventing her from moaning, preventing her from breathing as Donovan continued to lick and stroke her, driving her closer to the edge.

When her nails pressed harder into his legs, Davion backed up, only slightly, leaving the head of his cock on her tongue as she gasped for air, moaning with every exhale.

Belle shivered, and as her legs threatened to close to stop the build of her orgasm, Donovan's magic lashed out, forming two thick ropes at her thighs, prying her legs open. He looked at Belle for only a moment, shaking his head at her. This was for him as much as it was for her; it had been so long since he had heard her cry out, so long since he had last touched her, tasted her. She already tasted like ambrosia, but now, with the succubus magic weaving its way through all three of them, it was euphoric.

Her back arched sharply when Donovan curled his fingers inside of her, and Davion used that moment of a gasp for air to force his cock back down Belle's throat, rocking his hips now as she came from Donovan devouring her. Belle shook her head slightly, trying to pull back for breath, to cry out, for a full body release, but Davion denied her. The hand at the back of her head pushed her forward as their eyes locked; tears forming in the corner of Belle's eyes.

He shifted back at one final moment, and her hand replaced her mouth, gliding along the length of his hardness as her arms gave out and she fell to the bed, while the orgasm tore through her. "Good girl... Let us hear it." Davion growled as he leaned down over Belle. Donovan's vines of power slid back, caressing her legs as they vanished.

"Get up here and lie down, Donovan." That clever minx knew exactly what she was doing with that mouth, Davion thought to himself, unable to hold back a small swell of pride as his brother did exactly as he was told, lying on the bed. Belle shifted, straddling his waist while guiding Davion around the bed.

Her eyes closed, and another moan was set free from her plump lips, bringing both men to growl as she lowered herself down onto his shaft. Donovan's hands gripped her hips while Davion let the thick weight of him press back into her mouth. Looking down at Belle even as she settled on Donovan, he shook his head slightly, "Ride, Belle." Another quiet command, but Belle did as she was told, bracing her hands on Davion's thighs as she began to work her hips up and down, her weight easily guided by Donovan's steady hands.

With every bounce of her hips, every shallow breath blessed to her by Davion, Belle felt the power building between them; it set her skin to tingle, a thunder cloud rumbling deep in her chest. It was tangible, palpable, and swirled around them as freely as the tendrils frequently swirled her men.

Belle rode Donovan like a vision made of sin and silk, her moans muffled around Davion's cock as she bounced on her knees, thighs trembling with effort. Donovan's head was thrown back against the pillows, his jaw slack, eyes fluttering with every grind of her hips.

His hands gripped her hips tighter. Desperation clawed at his voice. "Belle- I'm-" His voice broke into a moan. "I can't- fuck- I'm gonna-"

Her teeth grazed Davion's length just as Donovan shattered, hips bucking up into her, his breath ragged and broken. He cried out her name, voice rough with reverence, as he emptied himself inside her. Belle trembled, her mouth slipping free of Davion's cock as she gasped for air, her thighs quaking. Donovan's arms fell back to the mattress, spent and dazed.

There was a beat of silence. Heavy. Waiting. Then Davion shifted, his hand tightening the grasp at the back of Belle's head. "My turn," he growled. She barely had time to inhale before he grabbed her waist and flipped her onto her stomach like she weighed nothing. The bed rocked beneath them. "You've had your fun," Davion said, eyes blazing down at her, as he lined his hips up behind hers, smacking her ass roughly once. "Now I'm going to take mine."

And then he was inside her. One deep, punishing thrust. Belle arched her back forward, her breasts crushing down on the mattress as she cried out. He didn't allow her time to adjust, or even to breathe; Davion drilled into her relentlessly, like a man possessed, determined to break and shatter. The hand that held her hair pushed her face down into the mattress, forcing her to look at Donovan as his chest heaved, still coming down from his own orgasm.

Her words came out short, mixed between grunts, moans, and the sound of Davion's body slapping against her, "Get... Over... Here... Let... Me... Taste..." She ground out before her eyes rolled back once more. Davion had shifted his hips ever so slightly, and the build toward her second orgasm skyrocketed into the stars.

Unsure if it was the compulsion of the succubus, or his sheer desire to please, but Donovan moved; Davion pulled Belle's hair, yanking her up enough for Donovan to position his cock just under Belle before he fell back when her tongue licked from the base to the tip; his cock twitched, still far too sensitive to the touch.

Her lips closed on the head of his cock as Davion continued to fuck her, their bodies jerking. Wild vines of darkness and plumes of smoke clouded the light from the room.

Belle braced her hands on either side of Donovan's ribs, her back arched, her body trembling from the inside out. Davion's hands bruised her hips behind her, thrusting into her with a fury that had nothing to do with rage and everything to do with worship.

Donovan lay beneath her, gasping, twitching, his cock still caught between her lips, sensitive to the point of torture. His fingers tangled in the sheets, his head thrown back as her mouth worshipped him, slow and insistent. "Belle-" he whimpered. "I can't- I already-" She moaned around him, vibrations dragging another helpless sound from his throat. Every thrust of Davion's from behind rocked her forward, shoving Donovan deeper into her mouth, until he was panting like a man being undone from the soul.

Davion's growl deepened. "That's it," he said, sweat dripping from his jaw as shadows curled tighter around her thighs. "Take him while I ruin you. Show us both who you belong to."

The moment shattered like glass, and with it, magic burst free in every direction. Belle let out a cry around Donovan, her whole body pulsing with pleasure and power as her orgasm tore through her like a scream made of starlight. Donovan's hips bucked once, twice, and then he was spilling down her throat again, whimpering, arching, offering himself with every broken breath. Davion followed last, slamming into her one final time and roaring her name as he came.

Shadows exploded outward, both men showing no restraint, but it was mixed with golden lightning. The room was covered in darkness, and the tiniest streaks of lightning crackled all around them. It wasn't darkness, it wasn't emptiness. It was a new sky; a sign of something magical snapping into place like a sigil. Belle's power had reached out and knit them together. Bone to bone, breath to breath, heart to heart, and soul to soul.

When the shadows receded, drawing themselves back into the men, they lay tangled together, Belle in the center. Nothing would ever be the same. Now they were bound; all three of them. Choices made together.

Chapter 21

Belle woke before either of the men... Her men... And ran a hand down her face, grinning while looking toward the ceiling as if they shared a secret, before crawling off the bed, doing her best not to wake them. Something felt different. It wasn't just a lightness in her heart of not having to choose; it wasn't that post sex glow. Something had changed. Finding the discarded robe, she wrapped it around herself before sitting at the ornate wooden vanity, so much of the wear and tear she had looked at on her face only the night before had already vanished. Grabbing the silver brush, she began to pull it through her hair when she saw Donovan sit upright in bed through the mirror.

Belle sat still, watching him process, his grey eyes shifting from side to side before looking over at his brother, still asleep in the bed with mild alarm, before they shifted to Belle, softening instantly. "Good morning, beautiful." He all but cooed, dropping his hands into his lap with a light, goofy grin.

"Good morning." She replied while turning in her seat to face the bed. Davion began to stir, and Belle felt a strange tug in her chest. Belle stilled, all three of them brought their fingers to their chest at the light pressure that felt like it was already there, something their bodies recognized, but their brains hadn't yet. Davion stood from the bed, naked, glorious, and Belle smiled, lifting a brow.

Now both men were ambling around the room, brains still foggy with sleep as they went about at least putting on their pants, and Belle just sat back, admiring them. But something still tugged at her, nagged at her, something was different. She pushed off the chair at the vanity and stood between them. "Do you feel weird?" She wrinkled her brow and waved her hands between the two of them, not knowing the words, not knowing how to explain it.

"Define weird." Donovan offered while buckling his pants before brushing his hair from his face, straightening his stance.

"Yes," Davion replied flatly while pulling his shirt over his head.

Belle shifted, pursing her lips while trying to figure out how to put in words the repetitive word of 'different' that had echoed through her mind. "It's like... I'm in my body, but also not. Like I can feel you. Not see through your eyes, not hear your thoughts. But I know where you are. What you are feeling. It's like we're... stretched. In three directions at once."

Donovan blew out a long breath and nodded his head rapidly. "I thought I was losing my mind."

"You're not. I feel it too." Silence followed Davion's flat statement, his eyes distant, searching for an answer.

"Ancient bindings," Donovan muttered, more to the air than anyone else, as if expressing it out loud would make it seem less insane. He pulled both hands through his hair now while he paced, looking down at the floor. "It's beyond rare, it's practically unheard of. Something from the fables and the storybooks..."

"This whole thing has been a fucking storybook..." Belle interrupted, pointing between the two of them.

"We didn't just fuck last night... We bound... The room... Our powers..." Donovan looked up, shifting between the two of them. "We are bound, claimed to one another."

As if she had been waiting for the opportune moment, the door flew open, "Oh, good. It's finally happened." Khandra clapped her hands together while brandishing a bright smile, gliding across the room to the three of them. Sadie was quick on Khandra's heels, but when Khandra came to a stop before the three of them, she made a quick shift and directed herself to Belle. "Get dressed. We have a problem." She crooked a finger toward Belle, "Bring that little dagger of yours."

Belle's jaw slacked as Sadie buzzed around her, pulling layers on, including a typical corset that was laced much more loosely than they had been in the past. "What is going on?" Belle whispered to Sadie, hoping for a quiet answer. Their eyes

147

locked for no more than a second, but Sadie shook her head slightly, not willing to speak in a room of royals.

"Throne room, as soon as possible, the whole trio of you." Khandra chimed as she left the room, a strange tone of glee in her voice.

The boys were in their shirts and pants from the night before, but Courtland and whatever little elf had been assigned to Donovan had given them both swords. With Sadie's help, Belle attached the dagger to her hip and the three of them made their way to the throne room, entering from one of the side doors.

Khandra met them as they came into the room, walking in step with them in silent solidarity. "The bitch survived..." A sour, venomous voice started before they were in her view. Queen Martine sat upon the throne, the second seat that had been Davion's for all these years, nowhere to be seen. "No one survives The Cathedral..." Her long, sharpened nails tapped at the arm of her chair. "Not only did you survive it... You brought back the mistake that should've been killed in the womb..." Donovan straightened his stance, hand at the hilt of his sword.

"Nice to see you too, mother." He stated flatly as the four of them came to a stop at the base of the steps that led up to the throne.

"This is why succubi were locked away..." She waved a dismissive hand between them, "Or killed... How is it that you got away?" Her eyes narrowed on Belle, chin lifting.

Belle looked between the boys momentarily, waiting to see if she had to hold her tongue and pretend to be proper. When neither of them moved, still as statues staring up to their mother, Belle clicked her teeth and offered a casual shrug, "Guess I'm just lucky like that?"

"You have poisoned them both, haven't you? You are a filthy, filthy thing..." Her lip peeled back, disgust evident. "Guards. Seize her. Kill the succubus. I want her blood on the floor." Donovan instantly stepped in front of Belle, hand on the hilt of his blade, ready to draw it.

Davion couldn't help but grin slightly. "Guards. You are dismissed." His dark eyes never left the Queen, not even as the

148

metallic clanking of armor shifted and faded with the sound of the guards retreating.

"You would dare..." Her voice faltered for only a second, "You would dare to defy your Queen?" She shouted at all of them; her sons, her daughter, the guards as they left, and even Belle.

"You stopped being the Queen a long time ago, mother. Just another old hag with too much power and the treacherous drive for more, and more." Davion shook his head, his tone dark and sharp. "You stopped being the Queen when you sent her to die."

Belle stood motionless through it all, having grabbed Donovan's arm when he stepped in front of her. Her only motion was small turns of her head, watching as the guards simply walked out at the quiet, simple command from Davion.

Suddenly, thick, sharp, black vines lashed out from Martine as she sprang to her feet, wrapping tightly around Donovan and Davion, ripping them away from Belle, leaving her exposed to the Queen directly. Khandra had warned her; she would need the blade. Belle took a deep, unsteady breath in and pulled the dagger out, holding it tightly in her hand as her men crashed to the floor, their bodies crumpling on the hard stone.

From her peripheral, Belle saw Khandra hesitate for only a second before rushing to Davion, hands outstretched, ready to mend what wounds she could as quickly as she could.

Martine used her magic to force herself forward, almost as if the vines were extensions of her legs, and she rushed Belle. With a quick step back in retreat, Belle was on the floor, and the Queen's hands were tight around her neck, the dagger knocked loose, clanging across the stone floor. "You will not survive this day." She spat in Belle's face while her nails pressed roughly into the skin at her neck, her air supply completely cut off. The black vines wove down the Queen's arms, no doubt giving her more strength than she truly possessed.

Davion climbed back to his feet, and his eyes went wide watching Belle. Before any of them saw her move, Khandra was at Donovan's side, providing him with the same aid. Davion's back arched as an ache in his chest tore through him, pushing him a step forward toward Belle. And Belle's eyes

149

glittered, the same golden sparks from the night before. An unfamiliar wave of calm and strength came over her as she grabbed Martine's wrists and pushed up with her hips, rolling the pair of them so that Belle had the upper hand.

Belle sat on top of the Queen, one leg firmly planted on each side as she began to pull Martine's hands from her neck, the golden sparks flaring at her palms, burning the Queen's flesh, causing her to recoil at the sudden sharp burn.

Donovan hadn't even made it back to his feet when the same pull tore through his body, and the sparks at Belle's hands ignited. Miniature bolts of golden lightning came from Belle's hands, and as she reared back and slapped the Queen, the room echoed with a low roll of thunder. She leaned down onto the Queen now, mimicking the Queen's motion, sliding her hands tightly to her royal neck. "They're mine..." Belle muttered, her voice hoarse, as she began to squeeze tighter. Another wave of calm came over Belle, and she began to pull from the Queen, her succubus nature taking over all logic and reason. "You had so much taken from me..." She growled while leaning her weight down on the Queen's throat. "You tried to have me killed..." Belle grunted and inhaled a sharp breath, the sparks flying from her hands, singeing bright red burn marks onto Martine's neck and face.

Martine's body started to slack, not from her life fading, but from Belle pulling from her. Belle's supposed cursed magic washed over Martine in waves, bringing about an unfamiliar calm. But for someone to have lived for as long as Martine had, and survived as long as she did, it was a mistake on Belle's part.

Vines snapped around Belle's waist and flung her backwards, her back crashing into the marble steps of the dais that led to the throne. Martine climbed to her feet, one hand at her own throat, "I will kill you... I will take it all, you worthless... pathetic... pitiful thing." Her free hand stretched out toward Belle, long fingers twisting as the vines wrapped tightly around Belle's body, almost cocooning her, closing in on her throat, bringing nothing but darkness. Belle struggled against the grasp of Martine's power, but the more she struggled, the tighter it wrapped around her.

"Mother!" Khandra shrieked, only for the purpose of distracting the Queen. By now, both men were on their feet and cautiously closing the distance between themselves and the Queen. Martine's eyes were red with rage as her head snapped toward Khandra. The seconds of distraction were all Davion needed, with the Queen's eyes off Belle long enough to throw a small, sharp blade at her, slicing the wrist of the hand that controlled the cocoon.

It faded to the ground, smoke falling to dust, and Belle gasped a sharp breath, arching her back high against the steps for just a moment before pushing herself upright. Martine's attention had already shifted back to her.

Both women lunged at the same time, Belle's hastened by the push from both men, their bond solidifying in her bones, giving her the strength and stamina to push forward.

But then the strangest thing happened.

Sound started to draw itself out, breathing slowed, the world around Belle decelerated for just a moment, a few seconds at the most, but it was just enough. Belle crashed into Martine, tackling her back to the ground. Every inch of her body that connected to the Queen pulled sharply, drastically, pulled for dear life. "You have doomed them all... Now they'll come for you... for the keys..." Martine ground out. She drained the Queen until there was nothing left but a husk of a woman. Belle fed from her so fast, and so hard, the Queen's dark magic betrayed her. The vines that once lashed out at Belle now assisted her, curling around her arms, bolstering her hold on Martine. The vines moved as if they were sentient, able to choose their wielder, and they were choosing strength.

As the Queen's heart took its final beat and stopped entirely, Belle cringed, flinging herself to the side, landing hard on the stone. She welcomed the coldness of it as she felt like she was overheating. That clawing pain in her chest instantly had tears rolling down her cheek as she writhed on the ground, feet kicking and scraping as if she were able to crawl away from the pain.

"Belle..." Donovan was on his knees at her side when she opened her eyes, gently trailing a hand at her forehead as she gasped for a solid breath. "You are okay." His face looked pained on such a minor level in comparison to the stabbing pain jolting through her chest.

For a split-second Davion hesitated; the last time Belle had suffered through this pain, he hadn't been fast enough to get to her, and he wasn't able to protect her through it. He crossed the room like a man possessed and fell to his knees at her side, wanting to scoop her into his arms and hold her tight. Instead of just taking her from Donovan, he took her hand, holding it tightly, but not roughly, pressing his hand to her chest with enough pressure to ease her into lying still. "Breathe, my love." He coaxed, and Belle did her best to nod.

A small elf materialized next to them, a grumpy scowl on her face; she waited quietly, not a word leaving her lips. Khandra stepped up to the trio and tilted her head to the side. "You keep what you kill..." She muttered, looking from Belle to the small elf. Khandra laughed then, wiping a small trickle of blood from under her nose, allowing all decorum to go out the window while she fell to her knees next to them. It had only been a few seconds, but she gave Belle that advantage, just like she was always meant to do, just like she had seen in her dreams a million times over; Belle was to be the downfall of Queen Martine so that a new queen could rise. "Gods, I'm tired..." She went from sitting on the floor to laying on it.

The ache in Belle's chest settled. The gnawing pain of her second kill now felt like an annoying bruise as she contorted to look over at Khandra. "What did you say?"

"She said that you keep what you kill... Your... Highness..." The little elf ground the words out, as if it hated the fact that it was no longer answering to Martine.

Belle pulled a hand through her tangled hair. "Fucking what now?" She sat up, crawling toward the elf. In the little elf's hands, a crown materialized, the same sharp, twisted metal and darkened gems that Martine once wore.

"You killed the Queen; therefore, you become the Queen. It is the law, it has always been the law, it will always be the law." Both men looked between each other and then over at Khandra.

"This entire time, Khandra..." Davion pushed himself to his feet, looming over his sister. "You had known this entire time it would come to this?" He bent at his waist, locking his hands behind his back. Khandra sleepily nodded and closed her eyes, extending her hands up to Davion.

152

"Carry me." She muttered, "I need to rest. We all do."

Chapter 22

Davion did indeed carry Khandra to her quarters, quietly questioning her about the extent of her abilities and why it had never been brought to light before. It was a secret their father made her swear to secrecy ages ago. If people knew that not only were they able to rewind time on bodies, erasing wounds, but that they could manipulate time altogether, someone would surely take advantage of it. If Martine had known, Khandra would have never known peace a day in her life. If Martine knew that Khandra dreamt of possible futures, she would never have been allowed to leave the palace; she would have been weaponized to serve the Queen's purpose.

She had fallen asleep in his arms in the middle of their conversation, and Davion considered portaling the rest of the way to her quarters, but didn't dare jar her around, not after what she just did for Belle. He deposited Khandra gracefully into her bed, pulling the blankets up around her before giving the small army of staff Khandra kept on hand instructions to make sure she was well taken care of.

He did, however, portal directly into Belle's quarters to find her pacing and ranting, throwing her hands in the air and then raking them through her hair as she rambled on. "She hasn't stopped..." Donovan muttered while sidling up to Davion, arms folded over his chest. "I sorta started half listening when she began repeating herself." He shrugged a shoulder and went back to watching Belle wear a divot into the floor with her back-and-forth.

"I can't be a fucking queen. What the hell do I know about ruling people? And what the hell did that raggedy bitch mean by 'they'll come for you' who the fuck..." Belle continued on, and Davion simply nodded, joining Donovan in watching Belle pace.

Davion took a small step forward, but his brother's hand on his chest stopped him. Donovan shook his head, "Just let her get it out, then we can talk reason, logic, and all things to come."

"If I've got the crown, that means I'm the ruler over you two, doesn't it?" She spun quickly, hand outstretched in their general direction, "Because you are princes and natural death would've made one of you the king, but I had to go and kill the bitch, so now I've got the crown... ugly ass fucking crown..." She shook her head and looked over to the bed where the crown sat. "And why are you glaring at me?" Belle bent at the waist, leveling her gaze with the small elf. "What even is your name?" She tried to edge back the bite in her words, knowing that none of this was the elf's fault.

"They call me Vel." The little elf replied, jutting its chin higher in the air. "Would you like me to polish the *ugly ass fucking crown*, your highness?" There was an edge to Vel's voice that made Belle's eyes go slightly wide.

"I'd like it to be set on fire." She exclaimed exasperatedly, not literally meaning for it to be set on fire, but sure enough, Vel looked at it, and it went up in flames on the bed, burning a hole in the sheets as well. "What the hell?!" Belle shrieked as Davion stepped up and used his magic to remove it from the bed, throwing it into the fireplace.

"Vel, leave us please," Davion spoke quietly while looking at the little elf, and nodded as they simply faded away. He turned to Belle, resting his hands on her shoulders, "You need to breathe." He gave a little nod, "There are a lot of things we need to figure out now, and I understand it is overwhelming..." As he spoke, Belle's eyes narrowed and her head tilted off to the side, "But the three of us will figure it out together..."

"Uh... Yeah... Excuse me... Who the fuck are you, and what did you do with Davion?" Donovan barked out a laugh, slapping his hand down on his leg.

He straightened and brought a hand to the center of his chest. "It's the bond... The bond turned him into a big ol' teddy bear." Donovan practically wheezed out. "We're all going to

155

bounce each other's emotions off one another, we're all going to... at least to some extent feel what the other is feeling." Belle nodded rapidly and continued pacing around the room.

It wasn't even the anxiety of becoming the queen and everything that entailed, Belle was positively buzzing, her skin wasn't itching, but it felt like it needed to be peeled off. Buzzing wasn't a strong enough word for the energy that felt like it was trying to burst from Belle. "Is it warm in here?" She asked while fanning herself as she continued to pace, stopping for only a second to look at the men.

Donovan took a measured step toward Belle, tilting his head to the side ever so slightly, eyes narrowing, "Are you okay?" He brought his fingers to his chest and started rubbing a slow, small circle where they felt the bond the strongest. He had thought it was just reality hitting Belle, he hadn't thought anything magical of it until her eyes locked onto the small motion he was making with his hand, she started to do the same, and a heat blossomed in all three of their chests; as if he had tapped into what she was feeling, and it was slowly consuming all three of them.

Davion shook his head, jaw tight, and stepped forward again. "She fed on a source of raw power," he muttered, more to himself than to his brother. "The Queen wasn't just a monarch; her magic was ancient. Twisted. And Belle..." He paused for a moment, trying to find a gentle word, "Belle drained her."

Belle stopped her pacing like she'd hit a wall, eyes wide and wild. "You make it sound like I'm some kind of parasite." Her lip curled back slightly while she folded her arms over her chest.

"You're not," Davion said quickly. "You're...fuck," his eyes grew wide as he could all but feel emotion bubbling in Belle now at his comment, "Belle, you're glowing." And she was. Not in the cute, flirty way; there was a shimmer to her skin, subtle, but unmistakable. The faintest gray smoke emanated from her, occasionally sparked with flecks of gold. The air around her charged like lightning about to strike.

Donovan blinked and then huffed. "Okay, so she's glowing and pacing and yelling and she's..." He waved his hands toward

Belle, motioning to the magic literally pouring from Belle. He looked to Davion. "She's overloaded."

"Overloaded?" Belle asked, stepping back, stretching her arms out in front of her, watching as plumes of smoke unfurled like a flame about to rise, reacting to her sudden panic. "What the hell does that even mean?"

Davion's eyes didn't leave her. Slowly, he tilted his chin down, the concern in his eyes shifting to something darker. "You fed on power. Your body isn't just storing it... It's *brimming* with it."

"Oh," Donovan said, his grin slowly spreading as he took a small step toward her. "Ohhh." Both men invaded her space, closing in on her.

Belle's gaze darted between the two of them. "What. What *oh*. I don't like that, *oh*."

"You will," Davion said, calm, clinical, like he was reading from a war report. "Your energy is unstable. You're going to crash or combust if you're not grounded. And the fastest way..."

"...Is through us," Donovan finished, taking another small step, voice lower now, amused and reverent all at once. "Remember years ago, those phones that exploded when the battery got too hot on the charger?" He motioned a small explosion with his hands before pointing at Belle.

Belle's throat worked around a swallow. "So, you're saying I need to... un...charge?"

"You're bonded to two powerful fae," Davion said, his hand flexing by his side. "Let us help you. We'll just share... ease that burden..." he licked at his lower lip, "Make you feel better..."

Donovan tilted his head again, a smirk tugging at his mouth as he gently touched the center of his chest where the bond still throbbed with heat. "Think of it like lightning needing a grounding rod. You are the storm right now, baby. We're just here to take the hit." Belle didn't move at first. Then her hands trembled. "Don't make me beg," Donovan added with a wink.

And then she surged forward, but Davion moved faster, bending low to catch her waist at his shoulder as he drove her back toward the bed. Her back hit the mattress, and she bounced slightly, laughing.

157

Davion reached up under the pillow and produced the robe tie that he had strategically taken the night before. "If you whimper, moan, or beg... You will drag us both under." Belle's head tilted to the side again, but she let out a quick yelp when black ropes formed at her hands and feet, pulling her body taut and flat against the bed. "Remember, this is for you..." He all but whispered to her while sliding the tie around her mouth, wrapping it around the back of her head.

"You're not stable enough..." Donovan was already pulling his clothes off with one hand while guiding his magic to pull Belle's clothes off. She lay on the bed in front of them, naked, bound, and now gagged. Davion stood back, a wicked grin playing at his lips as he admired the way she looked, so helpless but absolutely radiating power. He stripped down before crawling back onto the bed, bringing his lips to her neck. "Your voice is a fucking weapon right now."

Their hands began to roam, not greedy, not rough; worshipful. They explored her slowly, drawing power out of her with each brush of their fingers, each press of their mouths to her heated skin. She shivered when Donovan began feathering kisses from her knee, headed to her thigh, and bit down on the tie when Davion traced his tongue just under her jaw.

The bond surged, three pulses of magic hammering through the room like synchronized heartbeats. Belle arched, a strangled sound caught in her gag, her hips bucking involuntarily.

"We'll draw it out of you," Davion murmured. "Bit by bit." His hand trailing from the spot he knew the bond linked them, up to her throat, his fingers curling and urging her head back for him to nip at her neck

"We'll take everything," Donovan echoed from near her waist, placing kisses just at her hip. "Give it to us, Belle."

It took them hours. They worked as if she were a ritual; each movement deliberate, each touch steeped in magic and intent. Donovan was the first to coax her down, his lips trailing soft, teasing paths across her skin, whispering wicked things into her ear just to hear her muffled moans catch in her throat. He lingered, took his time, like every inch of her was a secret

158

meant to be unraveled slowly. His touch was patient and tender; a steady, smoldering heat.

Davion followed like a storm. His hands were firmer, his voice lower, commanding even when gentle. He knew exactly how to push, how to drag pleasure out of her with rougher strokes, his grip steady when she trembled, his magic dark and consuming as he anchored her back to herself. Where Donovan worshipped, Davion claimed. Both loving her in their own way, blending pleasure and pain.

They took turns drawing her higher, holding her in that electric space between too much and not enough. At first, she glowed under their touch, golden light pulsing from her skin as they worked her toward release after release, always pulling back before it spilled over. Shadows coiled around her wrists and ankles. Silken gags muffled her cries and caught her tears. They grounded her with their mouths, bodies, magic, and a power so deep it made the bond between them thrum, their pulses synchronizing to the beat.

Only when her body sagged, wrung out and trembling, did they finally let her break. Her last climax crashed through all three of them like lightning finding ground, the bond pulsing with a flare of golden light before settling into a gentle hum.

They bathed her, Donovan humming some half-remembered lullaby while Davion carried her to the water, steady and silent. She didn't even have the strength to hold onto him. They fed her small bites of fruit, wiped her skin clean, washed her hair, kissed her temples, shoulders, and knuckles with quiet devotion. And when they finally wrapped her in blankets and laid her between them, her breathing slowed, her hands curled in theirs, and her body gave in to sleep.

A faint shimmer still danced at the hollow of her throat, the final flicker of a storm survived. "I didn't mean to burn the crown..." Belle mumbled as sleep threatened to drag her under.

Donovan burst out laughing and dropped a kiss on her temple. "Of course, that's the first thing you say when you come back to reality."

Davion just shook his head, the faintest smile curving his lips. "You will have your own crown." He looked over to see her lips curl into a smile before sleep claimed her. The brothers locked their eyes for a moment, a shared silent breath before they nodded to each other; a quiet understanding and agreement; Belle was their future.

Chapter 23

The long, heavy curtains of Belle's quarters were all thrown open at once, the metal bearings scraping across the bar high atop the window as Khandra's voice roused all three of them from the deepest sleep they could ever recall. "Good morning, love birds, your highnesses, Queen and Kings of the Hightower Kingdom. There is much to do today!" Donovan hurled the pillow from under his head in the general sound of his sister's voice.

Belle grumbled and pulled the blankets up over her head while scrunching her body into a small ball. And Davion lay still, opening his eyes and glaring daggers at his sister even as she gracefully side-stepped the pillow as it flew by her. "What a rude way to greet your sister on your wedding day." She drew out the words intentionally and then let out the most beautiful laugh as all three of them shot up in bed, staring at her before looking amongst them. "What royal triad of crowns can rule without being unified?" She asked casually while waving her hands. Sadie came into the room, as did the personal servants to both men.

Belle's fingers came to her lips. Now it was anxiety; it wasn't the energy burning through every cell of her body. It was real, and the weight of the crown had her shrinking back already. Sensing her discomfort, Davion's hand clamped on Belle's thigh under the blanket, and Donovan trailed a hand through her hair, leaning in toward her to whisper, "Belle Hightower, Queen of The Hightower Kingdom... Gods, that sounds just as beautiful as you are." A light blush crept into her cheeks as she smiled.

"I'm getting married... Today?" At first it was a question, but she took a deep, steady breath while considering everything that had happened between the three of them, despite the constant turbulence, desire to scream, and there seeming to be danger at every turn; there was no one she would rather do it with than these two. " *We* are getting married today." She said more firmly, nodding and shrugging her shoulders.

"Naked boys get to leave; the women have womanly things to do. You are not allowed to see the bride for the remainder of the day, no sneaky portal stuff." Khandra pointed a finger at Davion, narrowing her eyes. "You three can handle being apart for most of the day. The castle has been awake since dawn, preparing for today. We have handled everything while you were fucking her to death and bringing her back to life." She let out a laugh, rocking from her heels to her toes, "It's almost like no one even cares that Martine is dead." Khandra watched as Belle shrank back slightly, "You'll be a better Queen for it, your highness." She added, with a grand curtsey. "Out, now." There was more authority in her tone this time, and Davion flung the blankets back shamelessly, grinning when Khandra cringed and covered her eyes. He turned and leaned to Belle, bringing their lips together.

"I guess I will see you later... wife..." The possessiveness in his tone sent a shiver through Belle.

Donovan wrapped his arms around Belle and leaned into her on the bed, squishing her under his weight as he kissed her neck and her shoulder. "I knew I would always get you." He laughed before clambering out of the bed.

The moment the door closed behind the boys, Belle was swept up in a whirlwind unlike anything she had been through. People swirled around her for hours; first were a group of people measuring every inch of her body from head to toe. She could've sworn she heard Khandra talking about a new wardrobe befitting a Queen; a wedding dress, crowns, yes, multiple, they measured both the length and width of her fingers for gloves, or for armor, Belle wasn't sure.

"I've always wanted a sister." Khandra admitted when the whirlwind came to a pause, she plopped herself down on the couch, the layers of the lengths of her skirt fluffing around her, "Instead, I got stuck with those two." Belle sat in a chair, and

Sadie stood next to her. Khandra wrinkled her nose up and waved a hand, "Just sit, Sadie, we all know what is to come for you." Khandra laughed lightly, Sadie blanched, and Belle lofted a brow. "You're going to get your very own court of ladies... sort of like forced friends... I scared all of mine off..." She shrugged and rolled her eyes, "How dare I be so open and progressive?" Khandra brought the back of her hand to her forehead, faking fainting, letting her head fall back on the couch. "All of that to say, I am certain Sadie will join your ranks."

"Girl gang..." Belle scoffed, making finger guns as she leaned forward to the table that was covered in all sorts of fresh foods. She looked at Sadie and nodded, "Oh, she's not wrong, you're stuck with me now." A tiny tear rolled down Sadie's face. She had grown up under the strict tyranny of Queen Martine. Servants were not to be seen or heard; they were trained in silence, and from the moment Belle arrived, she had felt a shift, and now that Belle would wear the crown, a flicker of hope bloomed in Sadie's heart, knowing things would be better for everyone.

The whirlwind resumed minutes later; all the measuring hands were back, carting in piles of clothing, and with Sadie's guidance, they were organizing clothes Sadie felt Belle would approve of, and clothes she knew Belle would rather set on fire.

Meanwhile, Belle was being delicately wrapped in the softest fabric she had ever touched. Two women helped her into the gown, a light grey that faded to black with golden threading in the train. To say it had a neckline at all would be an exaggeration; it plunged in a deep V shape to the base of her sternum, exposing a mark Belle had never noticed before. There, between her breasts, was the shape of a twelve-sided star, just a few shades lighter than her skin; a mark of their bond.

Sadie pushed the mirror over to show Belle, and her breath caught in her throat. She had worn dresses that were more expensive than she should've bought. She had clothes that fit her like a glove and were designed to stop people in their tracks, but there was something different about this. Belle trailed her hands down her curves, watching the way the fabric

163

barely moved on her arms, the way the tiny glints of golden thread woven throughout the dress caught the light. "This is better than I envisioned..." Khandra added while leaning against the mirror.

Belle's eyes drifted from the image of herself over to Khandra, "Just how much of the future do you see, Khandra?" She asked while being helped into a pair of shoes that matched the dress perfectly.

"Enough," Khandra answered easily while gliding around the room, "Father always told me to keep that information to myself, and though I do know you are a safe person to tell, I would be doing him a dishonor to break the trust in this gift he has given to me." Belle nodded, understanding. "Sadie will bring you down. I must go get beautiful now." She walked backward toward the door, "You look radiant, sister." Sister echoed in Belle's mind, making her smile at the thought.

Bells rang throughout the city, summoning everyone to the castle; along the edge of the upper courtyard, the nobles had been gathered and given seats with very little information; whisperings of Martine and the twins, and the girl caught in the middle of it all. Khandra came through the doors of the castle, walking up to the dais, front and center of the nobles, and overlooking the growing crowd.

She spoke eloquently of change and new beginnings and expertly weaved around the bombshell that the kingdom would now be ruled by three after this unification ceremony. She addressed the people of the kingdom as if they were equal and not lesser, something they had not heard from a royal in a very long time; Donovan having been gone, Davion being under Martine's thumb, and Martine just being awful to begin with.

As she neared the end of her speech, coached by each blood sworn elf, Donovan, Davion, and Belle all approached from different directions, meeting in the middle at Khandra's sides. They stood around Khandra, and when she extended a hand to them, all three extended their left hands.

Khandra placed a braided rope on top of their hands, "By this tie, we bind three hearts into one." With skilled grace, she began wrapping the rope around them, one thread dark gray, one black, and one glistened in the same golden thread Belle's dress had in it. Khandra nodded to them, and the three of them repeated.

"By this tie, we bind three hearts by love." She continued to weave them together as Belle, Donovan, and Davion all repeated. "By this tie, we weave the future of the Kingdom." Another tie, another echo. "By this tie, we will lead with strength, unity, and mercy." The trio repeated, Belle forcing herself to take a calming breath to hold back tears of joy.

Khandra took a step back, gesturing to The Triad to face their people. Three servants stepped up behind them and placed crowns atop their heads as they announced the last tie, "We are one. Bound by oath and love." The crowd went wild, screaming and cheering as Donovan wrapped an arm around Belle and kissed her deeply. Once he had drunk his fill, Davion took her chin in his hand and angled her head up to him, bringing his lips down onto Belle.

The three of them straightened, waving and smiling to the people, nodding and greeting the nobles as their newly crowned rulers. Davion and Donovan knew of the backlash that was bound to follow such a sudden upheaval in power, a sudden jarring shift in the kingdom, but they both knew it would be for the better, and nothing would ever be the same again; but as long as Belle continued to be their guiding light, the three of them were ready to take on anything.

The crowd cheered, the court whispered, and Belle stood tall. Internally, she was pretty sure that she was freaking out worse than she was before the boys... Her Kings brought her back down to reality. Her chest felt like someone had set off fireworks and panic at the same time. *I'm royalty.* She thought to herself, and the thought slammed into her harder than any spell or blade ever could. She was the same girl who fought tooth and nail to carve out a place for herself back in her own realm. The same scrappy bitch who threw hands with anyone who looked at her sideways in school. The same girl who survived foster care, bad decisions, worse relationships, and a life where she'd only ever survived by taking what the world refused to give her. She was the same girl who clawed her way through hell, literally and figuratively, and still managed to stand here breathing. The only difference was now she was a Queen, and she had an empire to tend to after, and a war on the horizon.

Epilogue

Her upper lip curled into a sneer at the sound of the vows. Pulling the dark green hood lower over her face, the petite redhead did her best not to scowl or openly show her disgust as she pushed against the flow of the crowd. She had to get out. Now.

That female. that outsider, a damned human, the one these fools would now call their Queen, had killed Martine. With Martine's death, the redhead knew the Holy Land's foothold in Hightower was finished.

Crumbling. Exposed.

These idiots didn't even realize what they'd done.

Her jaw clenched as she picked up her pace, slipping between bodies, ducking behind tapestries and pillars with silent, trained ease. She had to report back. Had to update her superiors on everything that had happened since Queen Martine last returned from The Holy Land. Taunting, arrogant, full of promises about how easy it would be to turn the empire from the inside out. All that work; years of careful infiltration, undone in one stupid girl's moment of self-preservation.

Queen Martine Hightower was dead.

And now, so was the safety of any remaining loyalists.

She shoved open a side door, vanishing into the torchlit shadows beyond the castle's walls. Unseen. Unheard. Just as she had been trained. The stupidity of The Triad had just been the catalyst in starting a war, and The Holy Land had far more numbers than the entire kingdom of Hightower. Their armies, their training, their discipline, none of it could be matched.

Certainly not by a kingdom run by a pair of pampered brothers and their little street rat queen.

Liraen couldn't think about the punishment that would follow for being the one to deliver the news; she would take it quietly, even if it meant being sent to the Cathedral for being the one to speak the words aloud. Her higher-ups would tell her she should have intervened, that she should have prevented the stupid girl from killing Martine. They would say she had failed her post. Failed her purpose. Failed Her Grace.

But Liraen knew better. Martine had underestimated the girl and paid the price. Now, The Holy Land would regroup, recalibrate, and come for what was theirs. This wasn't the end. This was the spark.

Vanishing into the woods outside the castle, she huffed out a breath, tossing one look over her shoulder as cheers erupted from within the walls. The sound clawed at her spine.
Fools. All of them.

She tugged her hood a little bit tighter, boots sinking into the forest floor as she slipped into the darkness. Every step carried her farther from the warmth and light of the celebration... and deeper into the cold certainty of the path ahead.

The Holy Land would not forgive.
They would not forget.
And when the ice finally cracked across this realm, when their armies marched and their magic froze the sky, when every loyalist was called home to serve...

She would be ready.

With one final glance toward the glowing castle towers, Liraen whispered to the night, a promise meant for only herself:

"Enjoy your crown while you can."

And then she disappeared into the trees.

Acknowledgements

This book would not exist without the people who nudged me forward on the days when I felt I had nothing left, and cheered loud enough to drown out every whisper of doubt. To everyone who believed in this story and believed in me, thank you.

To my family, who endured late-night typing binges, my "hold on, I've gotta write this down" moments at random times, and my habit of disappearing into fictional worlds without warning. Thank you for letting me chase this dream even when it meant chaos, cold coffee, and me insisting I was not going to rewrite that scene again. We all know I did.

To my husband, who came in like a knight in tin foil and gave me some of the most insightful feedback, helping me sew the plot holes closed nice and tight. I love you more. Now you cannot say I do not. It is written in a published book. I think that means I win. Ha.

To my friends, my council of chaos gremlins, thank you for listening to endless rants, letting me send you paragraphs at all hours, hyping me up, dragging me forward kicking and screaming, and refusing to let me quit. Y'all really are the backbone of this book.

To the newly named Mrs. Wheeler (hell yes, congrats babe!), thank you for your genuine hype and sincere excitement throughout this entire process. Thank you for sticking with me through this long, wild journey of getting this beast written.

Penn, thank you for all your hard work and for never once complaining about the pile of chaos I heaped onto you. I am forever grateful for your friendship, your insight, and your unshakeable belief in this story. I cannot wait to attempt to return the favor.

To Belle, the one in the real world, the forever hype-woman. Thank you for your constant encouragement, your steady support, and your gloriously practical "Hey, I have done this before" wisdom. P.S. Go read *When We Were Young* by Belle Shaw. It will wreck you in the best way and then stitch you back together.

To my ARC gremlins, thank you for taking a chance on me. Your support means more than you will ever know.

Finally, to every kid who grew up writing stories in notebooks, to the ones who have a billion half-written tales saved on their computers, or even ideas scribbled in the notes app of their phones. Keep going. Build your worlds. Create your characters. The world deserves the stories you are dreaming into existence.

All About Holly

Holly Crowe is a romantasy author, candle alchemist, and professional chaos wrangler based in North Carolina. When she is not building kingdoms or tormenting fictional men, she runs Pomegranate & Spice, where she creates witchy, hand-crafted candles and perfumes inspired by mythology, magic, and mischief.

She has been writing stories since she was old enough to hold a pencil, filling notebooks and file folders with worlds she was sure no one would ever read. Now she spends her days weaving fae bargains, morally grey love interests, and strong heroines who choose their own destiny.

Holly writes with the firm belief that stories should feel like magic: a little dangerous, a little seductive, and absolutely impossible to put down.

When she is not writing, she can be found drinking too much coffee, listening to audiobooks the length of small dissertations, and threatening to start eight more projects she does not have time for.

Connect With Holly!
(Please Do!)

Website: https://www.hollycroweauthor.com

Tiktok: @hollycroweauthor

Instagram: @hollycroweauthor

Pomegranate & Spice Candles and Goods :
https://www.pomegranateandspice.com

www.ingramcontent.com/pod-product-compliance
Lightning Source LLC
Chambersburg PA
CBHW030430120726
47903CB00003B/897